THE LEGACY SERIES

Series Titles

Kind of Blue
Christopher Chambers

The Clayfields
Elise Gregory

Evangelina Everyday
Dawn Burns

Township
Jamie Lyn Smith

Responsible Adults
Patricia Ann McNair

Great Escapes from Detroit
Joseph O'Malley

Nothing to Lose
Kim Suhr

The Appointed Hour
Susanne Davis

Praise for
Kind of Blue

"Skip the latest humdrum bestseller, and instead, do yourself a favor and buy Chris Chamber's gritty, compassionate, and wise story collection, *Kind of Blue*. I finished it feeling as if the man had left little pieces of his soul on every page, and I swear to God I lost count of the number of sentences I wish I had written."

—Donald Ray Pollock
author of *The Devil All the Time* and *The Heavenly Table*

"With the well-hewn solidity of windbreak trees, and with a rhythmic musicality, *Kind of Blue* transports the reader into the heartland's mystique, stretching from Wisconsin to Louisiana, and New Mexico to Florida. Here we find the edge and intensity of a Robert Stone novel, from a darkly humorous craftsman who can hammer down a story in a paragraph or let the pages roll on. Spotlighting those who drift recklessly in their minds or into an America seen at the molecular level, Chambers often begins with the minute detail and explodes it into revelation. I found myself compulsively reading on."

—Stephanie Dickinson
author of *Blue Swan Black Swan: The Trakl Diaries,*
Love Highway, and *Big-Headed Anna Imagines Herself*

"Conjuring the deftness of Denis Johnson and the yowl of Barry Hannah, these stories pulse with the heartbeat of forgotten America. They are lightning in bottles. They are dirt beneath the fingernails. They are broken hearts and open wounds, with just enough gauze to save you. These are stories that have been places and that will take you places. Stories that reawaken slumbering ghosts. They are stories that celebrate the extraordinary nature of our ordinary lives. Sidle up, turn the radio low, and have a listen."

—B. J. Hollars
author of *Sightings, Midwestern Strange,*
The Road South, and *Dispatches from the Drownings*

"These stories will stab you in the heart. In the good way, I mean. The way jazz does, and love, and butcher knives."

—Roy Kesey
author of *Any Deadly Thing, Pacazo,
All Over,* and *Nothing in the World*

"Christopher Chambers is a master of the short story and *Kind of Blue* is the proof. In this world of dreamers and drunks, loners and longing, the hopeful and the haggard, Chambers accomplishes what only the best writers can; he makes every character feel both universal and unique, each setting both a vacation and a return home. Fans of short fiction need to pay attention. This book is for you."

—M.O. Walsh
New York Times bestselling author of
My Sunshine Away and *The Big Door Prize*

"In *Delta 88,* Christopher Chambers showed himself to be a master of micro fiction, with characters and sensibilities reminiscent of Jerzy Kosiński's *Steps* and Thom Jones' *Pugilist at Rest.* Now, with *Kind of Blue,* he's brought his same poignant prose to a larger canvas, replacing that old Delta 88 with an array of wheels—from a glossy black rented Lincoln, a gray new Lincoln Ambassador, a Torino, Volvo, and Civic to a red Isuzu Rodeo, GTO, Camaro, and Buick Gran Sport—even a kid's pink plastic Corvette convertible. No matter the vehicle, with Christopher Chambers driving the narrative, there's nothing to do but hang on and enjoy the ride."

—Claude Clayton Smith
author of *The Stratford Devil* and *Garbage Cannes*

"The stories in *Kind of Blue* feel incredibly alive. Some of them make quick work with a blue blade, some sprawl out and moan awhile—others just plug in, light up, and explode. There's beauty in the wreckage here (and in the prose), as well as a dark, grimacing wit. This book shook me out of a benumbed state. I awoke inspired and energized."

—Michael Jeffrey Lee
author of *Something in My Eye*

KIND OF BLUE

stories

CHRISTOPHER CHAMBERS

Cornerstone Press
Stevens Point, Wisconsin

Cornerstone Press, Stevens Point, Wisconsin 54481
Copyright © 2022 Christopher Chambers
www.uwsp.edu/cornerstone

Printed in the United States of America by
Point Print and Design Studio, Stevens Point, Wisconsin

Library of Congress Control Number: 2022938354
ISBN: 979-8-9861447-2-6

Cornerstone Press titles are produced in courses and internships offered by the Department of English at the University of Wisconsin–Stevens Point.

DIRECTOR & PUBLISHER   EXECUTIVE EDITOR
Dr. Ross K. Tangedal   Jeff Snowbarger

SENIOR EDITORS
Lexie Neeley, Monica Swinick, Kala Buttke

PRESS STAFF
Rhiley Block, Alyssa Bronk, Grace Dahl, Patrick Fogarty, Ava Freeman, Angela Green, Brett Hill, Cale Jacoby, Hunter Keisow, Adam King, Jeremy Kremser, Amanda Leibham, Leo McEvilly, Abbi Rohde, Abbi Wasielewski

For Speed

Also by Christopher Chambers:

Delta 88
Inter/views
Ice Fishing for Alligators (co-editor with Peyton Burgess)

Stories

I've got my faults, but changing my tune isn't one of them.

—Samuel Beckett

On Montegut Street

Early on the morning of the day I got the call that my old good pal and drinking buddy Edward had died of a stroke at 53 back in Minneapolis, I was downriver, startled awake by a train in the midst of a dream. I was in a room with several people, friends and family. Bill Jr. was there, and I had not seen him in many years. I was glad to see him, and he seemed glad to see me as well. You got new boots, he said, and I looked down at my feet. I was wearing cowboy boots, and I supposed that he was right. I did too, he said. We looked down at the tan work boots that he was wearing. They were clean and new. I put my arm around his shoulder then and we stood side by side, rolling our ankles and admiring our footwear. I looked across the room to where his sister and the others were, maybe expecting someone to take a picture of us. I wanted someone to take a picture of us. We were both in good spirits and I didn't want to lose this. It was only after I woke up alone that I remembered that Bill, like Eddie now, is dead. I have this old leather tool belt I bought from Bill when we were in our twenties doing construction work and I was living with his sister. He was selling anything he could to get some money to get drunk. I used his tool belt all the years I spent framing houses, long after his sister left me. I brought it with me when I moved down south. It hangs on a hook by the back door, and I still wear it once in a while for odd jobs or working around the house. We all knew that Bill, like Eddie, had a drinking problem. Some ten years or so ago I got the call that Bill had passed out by the Mississippi River one night and died there in the cold. Edward was sober when he died, they said when they called, in a halfway house. He seemed happy, they said. And that's when I remembered the dream about Bill, and thought about the tool belt, and his sister, whom I have not seen for many years and of whom I sometimes think when the trains go past my place on Montegut Street, how she couldn't abide my drinking and how she said when she left for California that I had potential but was just letting it slip away.

Kind of Blue

I first read the famous poem "Sandinista" in 1984 in a new copy of F.'s book on a flight from Milwaukee to Boston. I was on my way to Cape Cod to spend a week with my ex-girlfriend and I was as excited to meet F., perhaps even more so, as I was to see my ex, who'd left me six or seven months earlier. My former girlfriend and I had met when we were students at a small state university that had once been a normal school or a teacher's college and had over the years come to specialize in animal agriculture. We moved in together after we graduated, me with a degree in philosophy and her in sociology and found ourselves confronted by what is often called in academia "the real world." We were ill-prepared to make our way in it. I found work as a carpenter, and she got a job at a daycare center. We lived in an illegal apartment near the freeway, barely scraping by and bickering constantly.

We lived together for a year, poor and uncertain of the future, struggling to make a living, miserable and taking it out on each other. We had a lot it seemed in common. Her father was a biker and a prison guard. Mine had been a boxer, which I figured accounted for the dementia and the bankruptcy. Suffice it to say, we spent holidays by ourselves, which at first was a pleasant change, though gradually she wanted more, and though I didn't blame her, I couldn't quite take the blame myself. We broke up, largely I believe, because we were poor and unhappy. We wanted more from life but did not know quite what it was that we wanted or how to go about getting it. I'd imagined that a college education would reveal a clear path in the world, a road away from the blue-collar life I'd watched my father struggle through.

I was haunted by my readings of Marx, which seemed to make clear the inevitability of my fate. The working class was not going to rise up. They were too tired or too drunk or too worried about paying the rent. After we broke up and I moved into a smaller and cheaper apartment closer to the freeway, I played The Clash loudly and often. But that was the extent of my revolt, with the exception of a rally against the first invasion of Iraq in which I marched on a whim with an anarchist drywall hanger I knew from work. We scuffled with some frat boys and suburban flag wavers. But I have a strong survival instinct, and I slipped away when the storefront windows shattered and dumpsters were set ablaze, before the cops arrived, and I went home. I had to be at work early the next morning.

Meanwhile the poet F. was in Milwaukee at the time, perhaps in a visiting teaching position at the university. I really don't remember the circumstances. Her young son attended the daycare where my ex-girlfriend worked. F. got to know her from dropping off and picking up her son at the daycare. When F. and her husband, M., a freelance photographer, were leaving for Provincetown, they asked my ex-girlfriend if she'd be interested in accompanying them as a nanny for their son. This was an invitation to a new world, a ticket out of the Midwest, and how she, my ex, came to be living in a house on the ocean in Provincetown with F. and her husband and son. I do not believe the house belonged to F. and her husband, but I don't remember now whose it was, or perhaps never knew, or how they came to be staying there.

Needless to say, my ex-girlfriend jumped at the chance to be a nanny in Cape Cod, which was a step up from wiping noses in a daycare for $5 an hour and distance from me. Norman Mailer's house, as I understood, was on the same oceanfront street. Many years later I took advantage of an opportunity to spar with T., a balding novelist at The Fox Head in Iowa City. Perhaps not exactly sparring, but a few punches were thrown before the two of us were thrown out of the bar, at which point T. clapped his arm over my shoulders and offered to buy the next round at The Vine. I shrugged him off. My right hand was beginning to throb, and I could taste blood from my swollen lip. He seemed almost jubilant, though he had a pretty nice shiner, or perhaps because he had a pretty nice shiner. T. was a graduate of a famous writing school there and had published a minor novel which had been acclaimed at the time as gritty and tough. There had not been a second novel. He told me that many years earlier, after the publication of his novel, he'd sparred with Norman Mailer, who was infamous for such stunts, in New York City. I learned that Mailer apparently fought in and out of the ring with many writers and celebrities including, legend has it, Ernest Hemingway. Or so T. told me in Iowa City. That's something, I remember thinking then, and it's something still, I think.

A month or so after leaving Milwaukee, my ex was lonely in Provincetown and she called me on the phone. I was still unhappy and poor in Milwaukee and we talked, and across the long distance it was as if perhaps there was still some spark there between us. She invited me out to Cape Cod for a weeklong visit.

My boss said I could have the time off. I'd saved a little money from a couple big roofing jobs, and I bought a plane ticket and a new copy of F.'s book, neither of which I could really afford. To be honest, I'd bought few if any new books or plane tickets at that point in my life. I think I secretly wanted to be a writer, and though I was writing in spiral notebooks at night after work, I did not consider myself a writer at all. I was a reader though, and that was something, I thought. I bought most if not all of my books at used bookstores and the thrift stores which was also where I bought my clothes and home furnishings.

So, I read F.'s book on the flight to Boston, taking frequent pauses to look again at her headshot on the back cover flap. She was striking, serious, and I wondered what I could say to her. Despite my college education I knew next to nothing about F., Nicaragua, or contemporary poetry, though I felt an almost spiritual devotion to the 1980 triple album by The Clash by the same title. So that was something. Sandinista! the album was my political awakening. Released in 1980, I embraced the band's surprising move to swerve from their punk aesthetic into reggae and ska and country blues and world music while staying true to their political righteousness.

I yearned to join the revolution, but the revolution was not happening in Wisconsin, and I had rent due and groceries to buy and a twelve-year-old pickup truck with bad brakes and bald tires. And so the months passed by, one like the other, days of alienated labor, vague resentments, cheap beer, weed, and *Sandinista!* I knew from my ex-girlfriend that F. was a writer and that she'd been in Nicaragua during the revolution, and I learned from the dust jacket that she was born in Detroit in 1950, ten years before I was born in a small town in the Upper Peninsula, which was also Michigan but its own place as well.

Upon arriving in Boston, F.'s husband M. picked me up at the airport in a battered Volvo sedan. I found out later from my ex-girlfriend that F. had, in a moment of existential despair, used the Volvo to ram shopping carts in a grocery store parking lot one afternoon, causing a small commotion in the town, though I imagine no more of a commotion than those caused by Norman Mailer over the years. M. seemed laid back and world-weary, a little disheveled in a fashionable way. I liked him at once, though I was at a loss for conversation. We rode in silence, listening to unfamiliar music on the radio. This was my first time out of the Midwest, and Massachusetts felt as if I'd left the country.

At this point, one might be inclined to think this is a love story, perhaps one with political dimensions and literary aspirations, and though that might not be entirely incorrect, I'll say here that this is not a love story in the conventional sense. In the end, I left Cape Cod alone, as lonely or lonelier that I'd arrived, without any glimmer of hope for reconciliation remaining and without so much as a glimpse of Norman Mailer. At least I think that's the case. It occurred to me years later that I could have at some point appealed to my ex-girlfriend to come with me to Nicaragua to join the revolution, perhaps with help from F. and M., their connections and advice, though the revolution was more or less over by 1984, and neither of us spoke Spanish, nor had much money. At the time, I could not even begin to imagine myself in Nicaragua.

The week went by quickly and without event. We walked past Norman Mailer's house, or the house that I believed was Norman Mailer's, each morning on our way to get coffee at a Portuguese diner in town. I watched for a glimpse of Mailer but there was no sign of life in the house. Perhaps he was in the city sparring with an up-and-coming novelist. I no longer remember how I knew it was Mailer's house. Perhaps F. or M. mentioned it. Perhaps my ex. Not that it matters. If I had run into Norman Mailer that week in Provincetown, we could have traded punches and I would not have had to bother with the balding novelist in Iowa City, though I probably wouldn't have passed up that opportunity regardless.

We went to the diner every morning, and I'd wander the town alone until my ex-girlfriend had a break from her duties. It hadn't occurred to me that she would have to work during my visit, that she was responsible for looking after F. and M.'s young son. I found the bookstores and made the rounds, but it was the army navy surplus store that I returned to each day to lose myself in. I had no money and so left empty handed. There was a vintage globe of the world spinning on a chrome stand shaped like an airplane. The seas were black and the countries, many of which no longer exist, were brightly colored. I wanted that globe, which costs an exorbitant amount, maybe fifty dollars if I remember correctly, but back then it may have well been five hundred. I went back to look at it each day and each day made the calculations and came to the same conclusion.

On what would be my last day in Provincetown, my ex-girlfriend and I went for a walk with F. and M.'s young son on the beach. We walked past Norman Mailer's house, which gazed out at the gray Atlantic with darkened windows. The beach chairs were stowed away along a weathered fence. It was the off-season and like many of the houses along the beach it was devoid of life. We walked out to a lighthouse at low tide with the young boy between us, holding our hands. I imagined that we were a young family, that this boy was our son, and I briefly felt something like happiness. The clouds were low in the sky, and there was no sun. Only the waves steadily bothering the shore and a cool, salty breeze ruffling the beach grasses that grew inland. The lighthouse too seemed to be abandoned, its door padlocked. The boy grew tired and began to pull back against our hands and drag his feet. Without thinking about it, I swung him up onto my shoulders. He calmed down and grasped my hair in his little fists. We walked along in silence. My ex-girlfriend wanted to head back, but I was reluctant. We were in a fragile moment suspended and good, and I sensed it would be lost when we returned to the beach house where we were staying. My flight back to Milwaukee wasn't until the next day but I could feel the distance between us already.

F. and her husband had gone to town for groceries and were planning to cook a meal for us. Finally, I reluctantly agreed to return. We turned around and began to walk back. The boy had felt light when I lifted him up, but now he was heavier. My shoulder and my neck began to ache with his weight. My ex-girlfriend said the tide was coming in and we had to hurry. I didn't know anything about tides, having never seen an ocean before, and I don't believe she knew much about them either. When we were living together in Milwaukee, we would drive to a beach on the lake and sometimes swim out a ways, but never too far since we were also always drinking in those days, which was another factor in our break-up. I have fond memories of those trips to the beach, the sun and the wine and our desire for each other, which was strong in those days.

It was dusk, and I could barely make out the shape of the lighthouse, a shadow against the darkening sky. I didn't realize how much the tide had risen until the water began lapping against my legs. My ex-girlfriend made a sound like a startled animal and began running awkwardly ahead of us toward the shore. The boy felt even heavier yet, and I could feel my feet sinking into the wet sand. The water was rising almost imperceptibly with each wave that pushed against my legs, and I could see that my ex-girlfriend was struggling to run. She stumbled and fell into the surf. I plodded ahead, unable to run because of the growing weight of the boy on my shoulders, struggling even to walk. She rose to her feet and shrieked again and began again to run ahead. I tried to run too but my feet sank into the wet sand, and the boy gripped my hair tighter as he started to slide off my shoulders. I fought to keep my balance.

The waves rolled in higher, and the sky darkened. There'd been no sun that day, and no sunset, just a gradual dimming of the bleak gray sky until suddenly it was dark. I could see some tiny lights on the beach in the distance and staggered toward them. The waves were not violent, not crashing, just steadily rising and arriving with what felt like the great invisible mass of the ocean and all the creatures in it. I struggled on and soon was close enough to the beach to make out the shapes of houses, black against the dark night sky. Then a big wave hit me in the back and knocked me forward into the surf.

I rose coughing and blinded by the saltwater. The boy was gone. I thrashed to my feet, flailing my arms, reaching out and turning, grasping nothing but water and air. I whirled around and called out the boy's name, which oddly was the same as mine. It was as if I were calling myself, as if I were lost. The tide continued to rise, and I could feel the swell of another wave. Then I saw a flash of white. The boy was wearing a white shirt! I reached out and there he was. I gathered him up in my arms and pushed blindly toward the beach. I remember the feel of the water and the sand, the smell of the salt air and the deep blue of the sky behind the houses, which seemed to stare out at us with vacant eyes. I was thinking only of making it to the beach.

When I finally stumbled out of the water and onto the cool dry sand, I dropped the boy and collapsed. My ex-girl-friend came running up and wrapped her arms around the boy. You stupid asshole! she yelled at me. She was crying. She and the boy seemed far away and insignificant. I lay on my back and looked up at the sky as she berated me. She was upset by how close we'd come to tragedy. She wanted me to think about what if I had lost the boy, what if he'd drowned out there. So I thought about it, and yes, it would have been terrible. It would have changed my life, our lives. It would have been a terrible thing, one that we would have carried with us for the rest of our lives. It was as if the boy was our child, the lost child we would never have. We found the boy but had glimpsed that loss and would not forget it. It would haunt me for a while.

But the boy was okay, she was soothing him, though he did not seem upset at all. I sat up. My heart rate had slowed, and I suddenly felt hungry. I wondered if M. had started the grill and opened a bottle of wine. I hoped that my ex-girl-friend wasn't going to tell them about this. I stood up and suggested that we head back to the house.

The boy was tired. I picked him up and he laid his head on my shoulder. I began walking. Our clothes were wet, and I was cold. He was heavy, dead weight as they say, and

I could tell he'd fallen asleep, but I felt stronger now, back on land. I would carry him back safely to the cottage. I walked, imagining grilled steak and red wine and a fire in the fire pit on the beach, and then a hot shower and the crisp expensive sheets on the bed in the guest room. Perhaps tonight, I thought for a brief moment, but then regained my senses. My ex-girlfriend had refused to be intimate with me on the visit, and realistically, my chances did not look good tonight.

I understood that we were no longer together, that she was my ex and I hers. But Provincetown seemed to me like an alternate universe, a place where the petty differences of our old lives in Milwaukee did not matter. Besides, I'd bought a goddamn plane ticket and a hardcover book to come out there to cheer her up. Though that was not entirely it. I looked up then and saw a figure on the deck of the house we were passing by, silhouetted, a shadow against a shadow, and he was watching us as we made our weary way along the beach below, though I could not see who it was or anything other than a figure. I could no longer tell where we were and had no way of knowing which beach house it was. A small red light appeared in the dark figure like an eye, grew brighter, then faded and fell away.

It was Norman Mailer, out on his deck smoking a cigar. I just knew it. I was exhausted beneath the weight of the boy but I wanted to call out to him, to call him out. Hey Mailer! To challenge him to go a few rounds. I stopped and as I stared up at the dark figure, the small red eye glowed again, faded, and then it sailed out into the darkness, tracing a thin arc of light in the night. I followed the light until it was swallowed in the darkness. When I looked back at the deck, he was gone.

My ex-girlfriend had walked on ahead, and I turned to follow her. My back and arms ached from the weight of the sleeping boy, but it felt good to have this burden to carry for a little while longer and good to know that soon I could put him down and be free of this burden. Back at the house, I would shower while my ex-girlfriend put the boy to bed and pack my bags for my departure the next day.

After I shower, I begin to pack. There's not much to pack. I pick up F.'s book, which I've not gathered the nerve to ask her to sign. I hesitate, looking once more at the back flap of the dust jacket, and then I pack it away. I join F. and M. in the room with the fireplace. The steaks are almost done when my ex-girlfriend joins us after putting the boy to bed. We're drinking big glasses of red wine, already on the second bottle. We sit at the heavy wooden table strewn with papers and manila envelopes and large prints of photographs of Nicaragua. M.'s camera, heavy and scarred like a piece of military equipment. F. pushes aside the papers and the camera and the photographs to make room for our plates. The meal is simple, unremarkable, and yet tastes incredible. The steak is charred and rare, there's a salad, a bowl of olives, and French bread.

After dinner, I feel drugged by the food and the wine and barely notice when F. invites my ex-girlfriend for a walk on the beach. I am sorry to see her go, F. that is, and I watch the women with their glasses and bottle of wine. F. places her hand lightly on my ex-girlfriend's arm as they walk out the door. She leans in and says something I can't hear. M. is watching me, maybe waiting for me to say something, or maybe just watching me.

They haven't paid me, or us, much mind until now, leaving us to ourselves, my ex-girlfriend and me. I've felt less like a houseguest than, what? The help's former lover, which I guess is what I am? I think about a guy I used to see shadow boxing at the bus stop. He wanted to be noticed and everyone ignored him. M. is a professional photographer, I think, and has seen the revolution. He has been a witness. I look at the papers and the photographs on the table, the dirty dishes, the bloody remains of the steaks.

I look away, at the stereo and a shelf of records. I ask M. how about some music, perhaps the first thing I've said to him all week. The wine has given everything a glow, and it feels like an ending. The Clash, I say, Sandinista! But he says no. How about some jazz? He puts a record on the turntable unlike anything I've ever heard before, something that I will learn years later is Kind of Blue and will in years to come listen to when I feel unmoored or tossed around by life. At the moment though, alone in Provincetown, I'm wanting only to hear *Sandinista!* and my mind goes out to the battered Volvo outside, and I wonder if the keys are still in the ignition. I wonder how much gas is in the tank, how long before my ex and F. return, and how I might find my way off this narrow spit of land and onto an open road leading somewhere inland west or south.

Meatcutter

The gray yards and slaughterhouses squat along the river on the flood plain where tractor trailers lurch single file down the pocked frontage road onto Highway 61 onto the rust-stricken bridge that spans the cold Minnesota. In the chain-link fenced gravel lot in the pre-dawn fog small red cinders burn like atavistic eyes inside cars and pick-up trucks. The first joint of the day, another cigarette with the morning beer.

We linger and then fall into the stomach-dropping chunk of the time clock, shuffle to the locker room into the reek of sweat and smoke and meat. Kill and Cut. We wear white in Cut, all knives and steel, fluorescent cold and dampness. Electric hum and belt whine, the relentless clack of tooth-and-chain pulleys, the nick of steel on bone.

They sway in from Kill on stainless steel hooks, halved and headless along the overhead conveyor. Nothing but hams by the time they cross this cold station. Every other ham trails a pig's tail which we trim with a neat wrist flick of a razor-sharp knife. The steel swings from the belt and every fourth cut we take it up, left hand chainmail gloved, one two three four smooth strokes to regain the edge.

The blade narrows over the weeks and months and years of sharpening into a sliver of steel as thin as the dim band of sunlight that cuts through the refrigerated gloom, through one small window near the top of the far wall. The second hand drags reluctant days around the clock. The mind stretches thin and tight as a wire as cold as these hogs passing by, processed into ever smaller pieces of itself into simple cuts of meat. The knife blade thins always sharp to a ghost of itself an ice pick a missing limb an ache a kind of hunger.

My Sylvie, Her Paradise

I was beat, my ears ringing, when I and the band boarded the tour bus behind the hockey stadium in Kalamazoo. I often have trouble sleeping after a gig and tossed fitfully, half dreaming as the bus rolled westward on I-90 through the dark Midwest, finally nodding off about the time the bus wallowed up in front of the hotel in Milwaukee. From the windows of the penthouse suite I could see the sun rising up out of the great lake, and I thought for some reason of Fergus. Last I'd heard he had moved back here to this, our hometown. Way back in the day, our dads had worked the same shift at the old Blatz brewery, drank side-by-side in the same tavern. We grew up on the same mean Cudahy streets. Baseball, underage drinking, garage bands, the constant pursuit of women. I watched the new day beginning and recalled other sunrises, a time when we were young and smart and with our lives still laid out in front of us like a long open road of two-lane blacktop.

The band was scheduled to play a big show at the arena that night. I should have gone to bed to get some sleep. But this was Milwaukee and the nostalgia had me. This was my childhood, my youth, birthplace of my desires and dreams. I resolved to look up my old pal Fergus. The concierge tracked down his number easily enough, and I gave him a call. After the initial surprise and awkwardness, Fergus gave me his address and insisted I stop by. I rented a big sedan and ventured into the vaguely unfamiliar metro area. Things had changed some.

* * *

See, I had last seen Fergus long before my fame and fortune, another life it seemed, a long, long road ago, before my stardom, before his marriage. Before his wife, and my broken heart. And after all that had transpired in the meantime, I found myself cruising the strange residential streets of his neighborhood, old feelings welling up in me like a string section, a bad soundtrack. I regretted the Bloody Marys I'd had for breakfast in the hotel bar, the little beer back chaser like old times. I drove slowly, like an old man, one stoned, lost, and haunted. I searched for street signs, a little bird in my temple fluttering. I reached for the radio knob, some loud young three-chord punks, snapped it off and drove on in the silence.

I had nearly given up hope, lost in a hell of bungalows and convenience stores, when I finally saw the street sign. I turned onto his street and counted down the house numbers block by block, then house by house. I pulled up behind a rusting minivan, snugged the luxury rental curbside. I chewed a powerful breath mint, and stepped out into his world, and hers.

A small mob of youngsters swarmed the yard out front, shrieking, the sidewalk a hazard of plastic-wheeled monstrosities. The scrap of paper in my hand trembled. I compared the numbers. The two-story ramshackle—its porch drooping in the center like an oblivious smile—1313 painted over in green with child-like brushstrokes that bled onto the alligatored white trim. No denying it. The same numbers on hotel stationary in the concierge's elegant scrawl. Cedar Drive, it read, though not a tree on the block. Overgrown hedges and sprouting, flowering plant-life thrived here in a chlorophyll madness. Only the lawn suffered it seemed, worn to dirt by toy cars and trucks, battle stations, action figures. The sweet, sickening smell of yeast wafted on the air. Milwaukee. I made my way to the door.

Standing there on the settling porch, I almost bolted. This is true. But I straightened up and pressed the lighted button. Inside the draperied hovel a small bell chirped. On the porch meanwhile, two dirty urchins had attached themselves to my legs. My designer jeans in saguaro white, relaxed fit, freshly laundered over snakeskin Nokonas. A middle-aged man appeared at the door, pleasantly unkempt and at-home-like. A blurry likeness to Fergus, Sr.

He waved his hand and the tykes let loose my legs, and with a joyous whoop they were off. The man chuckled as if amused.

"Fergus?" said I, incredulous. Balding, and shorter, he seemed. Faded Green Bay Packer T-shirt. An ample belly overtaking the waist of his sweatpants. Sweatpants? I'd heard he taught Civics at the local high school.

"Jackson!" The man grinned hugely, and I saw him then in the smile, my good buddy of the old times. The misdemeanors, the days and nights burning like roman candles, the teenage girls, the beaten path. My old Chevrolet, a primered bat from hell. And the natural wonders—the Grand Canyon, and Sylvie, the coroner's daughter. Sylvie slipping in through my cabin window after lights out.

Fergus stepped out and hugged me, clumsily guy-like but sincere. It was my old friend. An awkward moment. My eyes blurred some. All this damn pollen, I thought. I stepped back then, my snakeskin boot catching on a pink plastic Corvette convertible. I lost my balance, my footing, my cool. I was sprawled into the hedge with a leggy blonde doll thrown naked from her little car. I struggled. Pointy twigs rent my duds, scratched my tanned flesh.

"Jesus, Jackson." Fergus chuckled his old chuckle. "You haven't changed a whit. Always the comedian. Come on in and let's catch up."

"Fergus." I spoke up to him. The hedge had me, inflicting small pains and indignities. Children gathered and gawked down at me, an oddity in this place, suddenly the strangest man of all.

* * *

Fergus led me into the kitchen, a busy little room that appeared to have recently suffered a minor explosion of foodstuffs and crockery. From beside a box of Frosty Sugared O's on top of the fridge, he grabbed a bottle of Old Rotgut, swept clear a portion of Formica, and sat us at the table. He poured two jelly jars, several fingers each, and raised a toast.

"To old times and old pals."

"Hear, hear," I said, though my voice faltered. I was still unnerved by the hedge, the little naked blonde still lying in the weeds. I raised the jelly jar and tossed it back. Swallowed. Coughed. The eyes again watered. The old times.

We'd been cynical then. I, the sarcastic rocker in flannel and leather, an abuser of guitars, the Keith Richards death's head ring on my finger. Fergus was a poet then, a regular dancing, rhyming Irishman. In the dank, smoky Milwaukee pubs, he laughed his infectious laugh and said clever things, snippets of Yeats, and Dylan too, tangled up in blue, the girls all falling all over us. And now. What now?

"Fergus," said I. "You were my Moriarty. Whither hast thou gone? What's happened, old pal?"

"Life," replied Fergus, "has happened, as you put it so hiply. You old wild man, Jackson. Still single and on that wild, wild road. Still our Paradise, eh? Always the creative one. Rock and roll star mystic saint. You've got some stories, I bet, and you'd better tell them, every one, true or not. But first, meet the wife."

*   *   *

I choked at my jelly jar. I knew his wife, and he knew I knew. Fifteen years ago we'd parted in Tucson. The summer was up, the dull beatnik job with the park service, aching bright nights tripping around campfires, blotter acid, and the Birkenstock girls all flushed, pert and braless as sirens. Sylvie was one of those. We walked, she and I, the glorious mountains around us. We laid our gaze upon the stars. We talked. Our souls merged. Our flesh mingled. But then Fergus, my best wild poet pal. And Sylvie, my Sylvie. I saw it before either of them. The way her eyes sparkled at his antics. The way he antick-ed for us. For her.

I shrugged it off then. Free love, you know? This was the seventies after all. No time for dull monogamy and jealousy and such archaic notions. I found Candy, or Cindy, under the big, big sky. And Fergus my Sylvie. We all had a summer. Wild youthful gropings at the Grand Canyon's edge. Everything was so significant. My private ache so puny in comparison. I kept it to myself, medicated it with Cindy, or Candy, psilocybin and blonde hashish.

"Fergus," I said. "Your life. All these kids."

"Yeah," he laughed. "Ain't it a trip? Four of 'em now. And guess what?" He paused. I could not imagine what in my wildest. He yelled then, into the dark recess of the house, "Sylvie!"

My heart. I could say it stopped, but it did not. Lurched maybe. Picked up speed like a small plane laboring to take off and fly. But continued to pump, that hardy muscle. Valves opening and closing in turn. So lifelike and reliable. Of course I had known. I'd been invited to the wedding. A small, informal affair in a park in Iowa City. Very nice, I later heard.

At the time, my band, The Blue Centerlight, was hot, playing all the clubs in NYC. I sent my regrets. Fergus understood, of course, and Sylvie, I'm sure. And at CBGB's, I played my heart out, wringing awful chords from my favorite faithful battered Strat, as if I were killing it there onstage. I signaled the soundman to push my monitor way way up. Meanwhile in Iowa City, I imagined, barefoot Sylvie blossomed in a simple yet stylish white dress. The wind murmured in the leafy trees. And there were birds singing. Back in New York my noise was murderous. People swooned. Beer bottles broke on the concrete floor. I forced the guitar upon the amp. Oh, the distortion was painful and great. But even this I knew was old. The big footsteps of Hendrix swallowed my art, my petty shopworn pain. Fergus and Sylvie, pastoral in the Midwest, breathed clean air. Inhaled. He said I will. Exhaled. Me, too, said Sylvie. A few close friends and family clapped. A gentle patter like raindrops on a cabin roof. My hands clenched around its neck, I raised my guitar up, and brought it down with violence. I smashed it to pieces. I walked off and stood there looking at crowd while the shattered sunburst wretch howled its one unbending final note, its broken strings arcing in a monochrome steel bouquet. The crowd screamed and surged as if in carnal ecstasy. Women tore off their underclothes and threw them upon the stage. But I did not care. I saw through my sorry act.

Pete Townshend, sneered a voice in my head. Joe Strummer. I stumbled off the stage, my self-loathsome persona. And back in Iowa there was Fergus. And Sylvie. Standing in the great pleasant boredom of the Midwest, lawfully wedded, authentic, and intent on consummation. And a few close friends and family threw little packets of uncooked rice tied with ribbon.

*   *   *

So I should not have been surprised when Sylvie with child appeared in the doorway. I dropped my jelly jar. It made a dull and disappointing sound and rolled under the table, unbroken. No sharp shards. No danger of blood. Just this small puddle of Old Rotgut. I lurched up, knocking my chair over into the recyclables.

"Sylvie." I croaked. Then, "Let me take care of it." Meaning the puddle of Rotgut, the overturned chair, the scattered bottles and cans, her unborn child.

"Jackson," she laughed. Her laugh was the Grand Canyon at night—moonlit, deep and timeless. I fell into it.

"The same old Jackson," said Fergus, with his chuckle. I managed a sickly grin.

Sylvie stepped forward and touched me on the shoulder, her great belly reaching out to my hip.

"Sit down, Jack, please." She went to the sink and moistened a sponge, then knelt between us to mop up the whisky.

I admired the top of her head, the auburn streaked with silver. I ached. Her girl hands roughened from this life, her belly like an alien thing resting on her symmetrical thighs. I remembered those thighs. My own young head, alive. Paradise. I had to look away.

"More Rotgut?" asked virile Fergus. I nodded as if to say yes, please.

*   *   *

That time in Tucson we were young and alive but did not comprehend our youth, our life. At the end of the summer, Fergus and Sylvie quarreled. Our world was breaking up it seemed. Candy or Cindy took the shuttle to Phoenix to catch a plane back east to Vassar or Bennington. Fergus volunteered to stay and close up the camp for the winter. There was talk of Mexico. Fergus suggested I go with Sylvie to Tucson where he would join us in a few days. I need some time to think, he said. Big decisions, man.

So Sylvie and I went to Tucson. I had my secret hopes. We drove, she and I, in her Datsun Simplex. Technicolor Mexican blankets draped over the vinyl seats. Warm beer in a Styrofoam cooler. Bootleg Dead and Dylan tapes. All the hip accessories of the time. A great feathered roach clip from the rearview mirror showed which way blew the wind. Somewhere south of Phoenix we had a great, steaming breakfast in a little place with the menus all in Spanish and dark, trilling waiters—two heaping plates of huevos rancheros, gringo style with eye-watering hot sauce. We strolled, satiated, almost like lovers back to the car, our mouths alive and burning. We drove without speaking. Or spoke of things of no consequence, I cannot recall. The road rolled beneath us, the desert endless around us. The desert. Into the car through open windows, its heat and thirst embraced us each and we endured it together.

In Tucson we cashed our summer paychecks and drove a neon gauntlet of fried food, used cars and motels. The sun sank red and brilliant in the west. Again, it was significant. We ate cheeseburgers at Burgerland where I stole a plastic shaker of salt. At a roadside stand Sylvie palmed three fresh limes. The red sky bled into indigo, and we could not go on. I steered the Datsun into the Trail's End Motor Inn.

There loomed above us the lit mournful profile of a weary Native warrior slumped astride a horse, lance in decline. Air-conditioned. Free TV. I checked us in: a single room, two double beds. Next, I walked across four lanes of traffic and bought a bottle of mescal at the Liquor Depot. I walked back untouched by the angry traffic, feeling near beatific.

Sylvie emerged from the bathroom in a cloud of steam, wrapped in a little white motel towel. Her wet hair smelled of peaches. Her legs and arms were bare, shoulders bare. Knees. Feet, too. So much bareness. I looked away, turned on the television, glanced back discreetly at her bareness. I unwrapped two plastic glasses, split a lime in two with my Buck knife. *Vamanos*, I said, in my best high school Spanish. *Besame mucho.* I opened the mescal.

* * *

Fergus refreshed my jelly jar with Old Rotgut. Sylvie rinsed the sponge out in the sink. From the front of the house, children clamored still.

"Remember Tucson?" Fergus asked. "A turning point. A crossroads. What a time that was, eh, Jackson?"

Sylvie glanced over. I felt her eyes upon me.

"Yeah. A time it was." I shook my head as if in disbelief. In truth, I no longer remember what was said in Tucson. Sylvie and I drank the mescal. I wrestled demons—subdued the guilt of church and region, battled lust to an uneasy draw. Flirted first with Sylvie, and then alone with consciousness. I awoke sometime the next day on one double bed, my jeans and boots still on, the taste of death in my mouth. Sylvie slept child-like in the other bed in T-shirt and panties. I watched her sleep for a long, long time. A storm had passed, and in this new day, we were as we would be. Fergus's girl Sylvie, and their pal Jackson, their Paradise, waiting. Did we speak of it? Did we even know? When she awoke we went, Sylvie and I, to a sprawling flea market and wandered, bought worthless trinkets and junk. We loved that stuff and like roommates decorated the room at Trail's End, made a frail home of sorts.

Fergus joined us two days later. He joked awkwardly about us, loudly admired our stuff, the wreckage. Then he and Sylvie left me for the afternoon, to talk they said. I watched the television flicker, but saw nothing, the heavy plastic drapes drawn against the brightness outside, my mind in a mad daydream featuring Fergus and tragic accidents, and Sylvie and noble me.

They came back holding hands and smiling. Fergus insisted we all go out to celebrate. Celebrate what, I asked, stupidly. This, he said, his fortunate arms outstretched to indicate all, our lives, the sprawling ugliness of Tucson, the big yawning question of the future. Indeed. We went to a Chinese place with an all-you-can-eat buffet. We piled our plates and read Chinese horoscopes on the paper placemats. Fergus was a horse, Sylvie a dog. I was a rat, and I could not laugh with them, the noble horse and the faithful dog.

We spent a weekend in Tucson, living it up, spending our measly dollars on spicy food and cheap liquor, the three of us dancing together in the loud, loud bars. Two of us before my eyes becoming more alive. Then Fergus and Sylvie dropped me at the Greyhound and aimed the Datsun for Iowa. Grad school, a wedding, and procreation. I had nowhere to go and so followed the road, rode the dog west. In L.A. I crashed with my cousin for a while, found a dull job at the track and met a drummer whose brother played bass. One thing led to another and the rest, as they say, is history.

* * *

So now I've seen a thing or three in my time, done it all almost. Not quite a household word, but The Blue Centerlight just made MTV's Best Thousand Bands of the Millennium list. Oh yeah. And now the reissue, the Greatest Hits, the surge up the charts. And this reunion concert tour. But always and still there is this gaping canyon at the core of me. Unfilled, untouched by fifteen years, the women and the pharmaceuticals. So my therapist says. This grand hole in me, my Sylvie.

*　*　*

I jumped up suddenly and grabbed Fergus by the hand.

"Yes, yes, yes," I said. Perhaps a bit too frantic. My anxiety was rising. "A time was had by all in Tucson. More of a time by some than others. You know. I mean. Remembrance of lost bliss. Youth, desirous of everything at the same time… and speaking of time, I'm running short. A local radio spot. Poster signing at EarWax Records. Sound check. The usual blah, blah, blah."

"But Jackson," said Fergus, sidling up to Sylvie as if for a photo. His arm slipped around her so natural. Suburban gothic circa end of the world. They smiled at me, the two of them looking a little sad, confused. But beneath it all the undeniable happiness.

"Got to roll. Great to see you two. Relive the old times. Yes, the mad old times. We must again. Must do this." I tried to dislodge a business card, tickets from my wallet. The cards came out in a flurry, all of them, comps for the show at the fairgrounds that night—The Legends of the Eighties Resurrection Tour (seven bands on one stage!)—fluttered about the kitchen with stray receipts, currency, the phone numbers of stewardesses and barmaids.

A panic rose in me. I can't explain. The little house closed in on me, their fragrant, procreant mess. I ran for the door.

"All the best," I called back as I made my dash, "The expecting and all. This life of yours. This…life." I had no more words and there was nothing to do, as someone once said, but to get in a big goddamn car and drive.

*   *   *

Outside, the glossy black rented Lincoln gleamed at the curb, loaded. I stumbled towards it. I dodged the tykes and the hateful hedge. The power locks chirped, and I got in. Leather interior, dual climate controlled, tinted windows, premium sound. My shades lay on the dash, my trademark sharkskin jacket draped there across the passenger's seat like roadkill. My heart slowed to idle. I turned the ignition key. The engine purred its fossil fuel-injected thirty-two-valve symphony. The sunroof dimmed, I leaned back. A bank of clouds was passing overhead vaguely in the shape of Texas. I slid in a disc, something old and smooth and a touch ironic.

*   *   *

An old dead vocalist croons of true love as I pull out into the street. I must put some miles behind me, miles between us. As I drive, I keep my watering eyes peeled for a suitable windowless roadside tavern. I have a great bottomless thirst in me and hours to kill before the show. I see myself later tonight upon the stage in the leather pants of my youth, sweating under the hot lights, haunted by the apparitions of Fergus and his Sylvie as I gaze out over a crowd of aging rockers from Milwaukee and her suburbs, my fans and my people, arms all raised as if in supplication. And I can almost hear my voice intoning like the voice of God from the big monitors, speaking her name, dedicating one last song to my Sylvie. And I know that this finally is the end of it all, Jack, and then back on the road, the tour bus vaulting me across the plain all right, disappearing, it will simply be good-bye.

Scar Baby

The flaw was the thing, the draw, the raised imperfection, a poem of violence written on her face. She was what I might have called beautiful, though not a beauty, my best friend's sister. It was the crescent-shaped scar at the outside edge of her right eye that I noticed first. I couldn't look away, imagining the cut, the smooth skin of her face opening to reveal a glimpse of cheekbone or eye socket before the sudden flush of blood, and all so near the eye and its thick lashes, the paper-thin lids. I could not wait to touch it.

On our second date we walked along a quiet street after dinner and a bottle of red wine at a small Italian place. We stopped in front of a hardware store with an iron security gate pulled down over the entrance. She closed her eyes, turned her face up to mine, her mouth half open, serious. I reached out for the first time and traced her scar with my fingertip. Her eyes opened and she smiled. And then I kissed her.

On our third date she told me she had an idea. We drove to the marina where her father kept a boat. We brought ice and vodka, tonic and limes. We motored out into the teardrop blue lake. She killed the motor, and I dropped the anchor. We slowly undressed each other. We studied every scar, the magnificent and the barely perceptible, told their stories in detail. We inhaled the fumes of alcohol and lake and gasoline, tasted these things on each other's skin. As the sun dropped into the dark, lush shoreline where lights in expensive homes were flickering on like fireflies, I tripped barefoot over a tackle box and spilled its contents across the bottom of the boat. She glowed in the last reflected light of the day, kneeling in the mess of hooks and lures. She held out to me a slender pearl-handled filet knife sheathed in leather. A memento? she said.

Take the Wheel

I'd been days without conversation. Simple exchanges at convenience stores and truck stops, roaming freeways and cities strange to me on a lonely sabbatical of sorts. Just driving, drifting, seeing what I could see, deep into the heart of the vague Midwest. Okay. I'd departed my soon-to-be-ex-wife, a household, twenty years of quality consumer goods and the company retirement plan. I packed a bag and left the rest. Let's say I woke up from my slice of the American Dream, unrested. Beyond restless. Driven over an edge I'd never known was yawning there so close. Lost it, the way it looks. An accumulation of small indignities reaching critical mass: an unfaithful wife and all that primal heartache, the general lack of common courtesy on the road, the inexorable digital blink of time, et cetera. And too I'd recently reached the age of my father's suicide. And so on. And so now.

In Toledo I left the car in a parking ramp and walked. I had a need for fresh air, and to feel my feet again in contact with this spinning earth. I walked, conscious of my steps and my breathing. I recalled this Hollywood truism: The more you drive the less you think. I'd been driving a long, long time.

I walked up a cracked and canted sidewalk, leaning into the landscape of the place, its pedestrian decay. This the home of paper mills and pharmaceuticals and of the Gibson SG solid body electric, the desired guitar of my youth. On my left, cars rushing past. On my right, vacant businesses and the gaping hole of a demolished building, a big emptiness, a border of plywood fence papered with posters of rock and art, all insistent repetition. I glanced as I passed. The stylish images of sex and violence thrilled me, and then too I felt the old sick guilt. We are animals, I thought, and cursed with this soul. Then an animated young man appeared suddenly beside me, in stride with me. He tentatively touched my arm.

"What do you want?" he said, his voice soft as a priest. His clothes seemed to belong to someone larger than he, the expensive sneakers flashed with each step. His complexion was bad, his manner practiced and smooth. He mumbled some euphemistic list.

So convincing, his sincerity. But I had been around a block or two and knew of the world both firsthand and by hearsay. I'd learned hard lessons in my time. I wore a long dark coat, somber but elegant. In the plate glass of a vacant bookseller's down the street I'd seen my reflection. A gentleman in slight decline, graying temples, yesterday's whiskers. A man without a woman. Unseen beneath the coat the handgun nestled in my waistband. Warm, solid, shiny, and loaded. Reassuring. Yeah, the whole Freudian thing. But only for self-defense, I swear. I am not a violent man.

"Why would you care what I might want?" I replied without breaking my stride.

He kept pace and repeated, "What do you want?" And softly again, "What do you want?"

The query annoyed me, its crow-like repetition. It's false goodwill. It struck me. Here I was, hundreds of miles from the place I'd called home, gone without a trace, only to have this street punk quiz me on my wants and desires. I'd had it all: a wife, a job, a sense of purpose. Trials the likes of which he could not imagine. The firearm beckoned me softly. I walked on stoic, ignored the youth, considered my options. He mumbled on as we walked side by side, the air between us charged. But then up ahead. At the corner stood two uniformed policemen, sipping coffee at a kiosk, scanning passersby with a predatory gaze, heavily armed, musclebound in navy blue. The law. My uninvited companion turned suddenly and disappeared. I continued alone and at the corner passed the two closely. There were other pedestrians about, a bus disgorging. I brushed past the taller cop, apologized.

"Pardon me," said I. Proper diction, eyes downcast as in deference. A true gent. He nodded, only slightly annoyed, and made a small step aside. I continued on to the parking ramp. I wondered once again about the Orson Welles character, as I had dubbed him, a large man in a dark suit whom I came to believe had followed me across two states. He haunted me now and then.

He'd always carried a newspaper and chewed on an unlit cigar. What had he wanted? Okay, I'd finally snapped. The terrifying possibilities I imagined. I know how these things always end. The doggedness of his subtle pursuit suggested private investigation. Hired by my soon-to-be-ex? Her suave personal fitness trainer? What more could they want from me? I could not bear to find out.

I circled back on him shadowing me, a TV cop show move. I left him near a roadside historical marker commemorating a minor skirmish in the War Between the States. The gunshot was so small in that great dusky space, like the yip of a lap dog in a coliseum. And yet, there lay Welles lifeless. Not at all like in the movies. An awful sickness in my chest.

I rolled his heavy body over a brushy embankment unseen. He was some kind of a burden. A good part of me went over with him, I soon realized. Whoever he was.

* * *

Back behind the wheel, I sat at a stoplight. Ah, Kalamazoo. Well-dressed men and women scurried in and out of office buildings, crossed in the crosswalks unsmiling, clutching fine leather briefcases and cellular phones. All around me all intent on business of great importance. And I? What should I do? What did I want? I had left behind all that was important and had become like a stranger to the man I had been. I had crossed lines. The car was large and expensive, a new Lincoln Ambassador grayish in color, and in it I felt large. Invisible. Safe almost. I did not own the car of course, could not have paid for it. And yet with a credit card and the proper demeanor, I had been handed the keys by a bored young man at a rental agency in a city much like this one. Leather seats like an Italian sofa, the finest in stereo sound, a computer with internet access. Satellite tracking system. I knew always where I was, if not ever why.

I put the transmission in park and slid over to the passenger's seat. A new perspective. So calming here on the right. Over there the driver's seat, proverbial and actual. The wheel.

"Take the wheel," I said aloud, to myself or to someone yet unknown to me. "Oh, where is the autopilot in this machine?" I was listening to talk radio, a local call-in show. The topic was ostensibly the coming hard times, the decline and fall. Apocalypse soon. Everyone had their fears and complaints. Then a woman's voice arrested me.

"Where have all the good men gone?" The pain in her voice was palpable, sublime.

"What do you want?" I asked. The woman, the car, myself. Car horns honked. The stoplight had turned green. I could see it sway gently above the street like an unblinking eye, stretched out across the seats, as I was, my head on the passenger's armrest. The unaverted gaze. Like Gatsby's Dr. Eckleburg, maybe, keeping vigil. I asked again. "What do you want?"

Back in high school English my brain raced on lust to the detriment of all else. I recall little more than the painful, unrequited desire, the blossoming Daisy's about me. Yet I still believed in the green light, a fine orgastic future receding. I had not slept in days, and the feeling is hard to describe. Automobile horns honked a while, and then there was silence.

* * *

I drove out of the city with other cars, absently followed a white European sedan exiting the highway, down a frontage road, and onto a wide drive that led to a stately, secluded manse. A tasteful sign proclaimed it Fine Dining. More drawn than hungry, I followed on and parked the Lincoln in a landscaped lot. I could not stop myself it seemed. I followed a well-dressed couple into the building. Red carpet, oak door, beveled windows, polished brass hardware, a parlor with a doorman. I kept on my long coat, peered into a room where young men in tuxedos whirled about, serving. Cut glass pitchers of cold water, silver carafes of coffee, and great silver trays of fresh bread and glistening pastries. Sunday brunch, once my favorite meal, a weekly extravagance for my wife and me. I felt a sudden pang.

In my nostalgia, I witnessed a fetching woman ahead of me, one of a party of three, gracefully swipe a pastry from one of the large silver platters without missing a step. She took a bite as she glided down the stairs, her companions chattering around her. A vision to me. Her self-consciousness becoming, a shy and careful beauty. I, emboldened by her insouciance, grabbed a chocolate donut and followed them, her, into the bar.

Our eyes met, clichéd as it may sound, in that dim interior, both of us savoring a last mouthful of pastry, evidence of crumbs upon our lips. Her hand went to her mouth, guilty yet demure. The gesture broke my heart. I smiled as if to say "It's all right. I too stole a pastry. I think you are beautiful in this light, and I'm not such a bad guy. Really."

She sat at a table with her companions. They ordered drinks, and again our eyes met across the room, this time a significant duration, and I thought, the hint of invitation. I composed myself as best I could, a hand through my hair, a healthy swallow of scotch. I stood tall, breathed deep.

I approached with confidence I did not truly have and asked if I might join them. They looked at each other rapidly in turn. Such nonverbal communication. I marveled as they came to a silent consensus, the pretty pastry thief wordlessly interceding on my behalf. "Sara," she finally said, and offered me her hand, cool and thin, with a light dusting of confectioner's sugar.

Her pals had names less memorable, a woman and a man, both friendly enough. I introduced myself as a screenwriter from New Orleans. It might be true, I thought. "I'm scouting locations for a new feature, a comic drama, millennial Everyman angst, think *Death of a Salesman* meets *Natural Born Killers*."

Then the usual chitchat, all of us doing passably well at first. I almost told them I'd lived in this city years ago as a child. The military school, my apocryphal youth. Grew up here as it were. But it seemed not quite true.

That morning I had driven past the site of George S. Patton Academy. Gone. A vast expanse of asphalt, a parking attendant's booth where once had stood a great red brick institution of Catholic education, corporal punishment. My portrait as a small boy. The smells of chalk dust, floor wax, shoe polish, and vomit. Elmer's glue. So lost in memory, I did not hear Sara's question. Something about reading.

"Do I read?" I repeated. She became embarrassed. Had there been an unintended rebuke in my tone? She seemed to admonish herself. "Oh, no. I do, and a reasonable question." The color in her cheeks caused a flush in mine. I hastened to reassure her. "It's all my fault. I haven't spoken in days. You forget how after a while." I looked to the others in hope. "You know how it is." They nodded carefully. I was scaring them some.

"I've read 'em all." I tried to achieve an amicable tone. "Dostoevsky, Beckett, Joyce. The thing is, it's all made up, our lives, all fiction. We can do what we want. Be whomever. Or not." I could lock the gun in the glovebox. I could throw it in the river. There was a rank-smelling river here, wasn't there? I thought. I had crossed it only yesterday. Or had that been Toledo?

I longed to tell Sara that I'd heard her on the radio, been wounded by her voice. And that I shared her concern about where go the good. I simply longed. But where to from here?

I knew what I wanted now, to move on to later in the evening when we would be at last alone together in her modest apartment, slightly tipsy from a nice California pinot or merlot. Kissing like teenagers. Easy listening on low, the music of our parents suddenly honest and painfully true. How could this come to pass?

First, she in the Lincoln, I behind the wheel, the inevitable drive. On the way, our tentative conversation, the headlights searching.

"I don't ordinarily…" she would begin to say. But I would already know. She's not the kind of girl, ordinarily, to be carried away into a carnal embrace with a stranger, to confess her deepest itch and the desire to scratch it. But I already knew this. I would firmly insist I sleep on the sofa this first night. On the sofa, from where I could hear her peaceful breathing down the hall, and watch the long, strange shadows cast upon the walls by streetlight or moon.

"There is something to proving one's self honorable," I would say at that crossroads of our night. "Something to pleasure deferred. Absence, fondness, and the heart, you know."

I'm sure Ted Bundy was one charming motherfucker, an All-American boy. Never a night on the sofa for Ted. It's a dangerous world for the pretty things. This is where I take my stand against the darkness and its charm.

I can see it all clearly. I'll start over with Sara. Her friends, what're their names, will be my friends. I will make this city mine, again. A great comeback story. The underdog finds true love. I will love this woman as she deserves to be loved, now that I know how, having learned the hard way the ways of the heart. I see us very near in an old station wagon, a third-floor walk-up, Saturday matinees. In the evening I make pasta and a salad. I pour the wine. Sara poses laughing in only heels and faux pearls, repeated in a thrift store mirror, my goddess, our funhouse, the queen size mattress sporting cartoon sheets…but just now I'm tired. The lullaby hum of the freeway, faraway sirens from another world. Sara, my love, you take the wheel. We are almost there.

The Velvet Underground

The name was lifted from an old book on sadomasochism. Warhol's idea, I heard, but all before my time. I discovered late the repetition of soup cans, the Sticky Fingers zipper, the banana. Sweet Jane and Heroin were once the soundtrack of my life. But my band never made it out of the garage.

Years later I meet a girl from Czechoslovakia from the same village as Warhol's parents. A distant cousin to the artist, eighteen and shy, freckled, Ingrid appeared from another world with her backpack and child-like English. I was the nice American guy offering my apartment. We listened to albums all night long, and when we talked it was slow and simple. I explained our imminent fame, fifteen minutes worth each at least.

With the sunrise we rode my motorcycle to a café, and then out of the city onto long twisting country roads, caffeine rushing through our veins, throttle wide open, flesh and machine synchronized, her arms tight around my waist for miles without words, her chest against my back, leather on leather, only the whip of the wind and the howl of the motor rising up behind us. I wanted to ride on into the night with her wrapped around me. I'd given her my bed and slept on the sofa, hoping she might invite me in. She did not, and when she left I returned to rock and roll and the raw guitars. And it was all right, I sang along.

For months after I would find Brillo boxes, electric chairs, Marilyn, and Mao in my mailbox. I savored the ache, the postcards from Chicago, New York, and Berlin trailing behind her like footprints, her fresh and stilted English in deep blue ink asking about my life and was I famous yet.

Best Western

In those days, truth be told, I was at McCready's, one side of the bar or the other, most every night. After my shift ended on the loading dock, I'd wander down the street to McCready's whether I was working the bar or not. My day job was Hamsun Press, a small publisher of large architectural books, where I worked shipping and receiving. I packed books into boxes all day, boxes onto pallets. I drove a forklift stacking pallets of boxes of books onto trucks. I liked to say in those days, to anyone who'd listen, that I was in publishing. I tended bar part-time at the pub, one or three nights a week. I was biding my time at that point, waiting I guess for something to happen.

So one evening at bar time, having nothing in particular to do and nothing waiting for me at home besides an ex-library copy of Moby Dick I'd been trying to wade through since stumbling upon it at the Goodwill, I overheard a couple of defense lawyers talking during happy hour about a warehouse party nearby that night. They'd loosened their neckties and were drinking good gin. I took note of the details. I knew the neighborhood and could picture the building. November can be a cruel, cruel month in Minneapolis, the days becoming brutishly colder and shorter, the nights long and bitter. November in Minneapolis you take your solace when and where you can.

Later that night after closing the bar I made my way to the party. The warehouse was nearby, down by the river, six or seven stories of gentrified brick that looked to me a lot like going to work. Shortly I was rattling up five stories into this warehouse in a freight elevator that smelled of machine oil with some fashionably dressed strangers, two couples, and me, some guy in work boots. When it jerked to a stop they stood there, waiting I guess for the door to open. I reached down and yanked the wooden safety gate up by the canvas strap, slid the metal gate open and stood aside. They stepped carefully out, gazes averted, and I followed them into the party.

In no time I was nursing a beer at the edge of a small crowd, taking stock of the scene. The party consisted of a lot of people I didn't know gesturing and talking loudly in this loft outfitted with exposed brick and a few pieces of low-slung modern furniture. Original artwork it appeared on the walls. Dance music thumped from somewhere through speakers, *Meat is Murder*, I recall. This was the eighties, and I could feel the insistent bass in my chest cavity. I was no wise guy despite how it might have looked. I wasn't looking for trouble. I wasn't looking to get tangled up in anything. I guess though when I saw her I had an idea, to be honest, right from the get-go of what I might be getting myself into.

I glimpsed her at the other edge of the crowd, draped over a white leather Barcelona chair, looking vaguely famous. Even from that distance I could tell she was all kinds of trouble, so I knew what I was flirting with. There was a guy standing beside me in a rumpled suit who looked like he hadn't slept or shaved in three days. I pointed her out and asked if he knew who she was. As I'd suspected, he did, and I gleaned an interesting detail. It seemed her boyfriend was doing time in a federal pen up north. This was, or so it seemed to me at the time, fortuitous, the boyfriend temporarily out of the picture for the time being. I finished my beer. This, I recall thinking, meaning her, could be a nice little fling, no harm, a temporary thing to pass the time. I had a couple more, watching her while I drank.

When I felt ready, I shouldered my way into the crowd. I worked my way through the bodies and the chatter and appeared finally there beside her. It was no small effort. She did up close look like trouble, I saw. Even more so up close. I liked her proximity. I wanted her badly. I said something to her by way of introduction. She appeared unimpressed, cool, hostile almost, but I'd been drinking and so persisted in conversation way out of my character.

I persisted and at some point later, in the early hours of morning she agreed, to my surprise, to let me drive her home. So I drove her home. When I asked if I might come up for a nightcap or coffee, she said I don't think so. I got out of the car and walked her to the door, dogged her into the building nonetheless. In the lobby she told me she was too tired but seemed mildly amused at my persistence. She stepped into the elevator, and I followed. You can come up, she said, but I'm not going to fuck you. And then she said, seven.

That's all right, I said, and for the first time of many times to come, I pressed my finger on the button for the seventh floor, and the small red light at the center of it lit up. She might have been ignoring me until the moment, as we were being elevated up, I got down on my knees more or less spontaneously and buried my face into her midsection and breathed in deeply, nothing but two thin layers of musky fabric momentarily between us. It felt like the only thing to do at the time. In retrospect I realize we both must have been intoxicated and lonely. As we passed the third floor she placed her hands on my head. I felt comforted, and in this way, in this sort of awkward embrace, we ascended into her building, to the seventh floor, up into the complications in which we would soon become entangled.

* * *

Late one morning months later over coffee Caroline announced that she wanted to visit her boyfriend Geoffrey who was in fact incarcerated in a prison outside of Duluth doing three to five for conspiracy to distribute Class A narcotics. I had never met Geoffrey, who long before I made her acquaintance, had given Caroline an unruly English Sheepdog that hated me. I did not much care for it either, though I might have almost felt sorry for it if not for its hostility toward me. I never was able to quite feel comfortable in her apartment. The dog was high strung, in part due to the fact, I suspect, that it couldn't see well for the shaggy fur hanging over its eyes.

Whenever Caroline went out, she locked the dog into one of the bedrooms of her two-bedroom apartment that overlooked a park from up on the seventh floor of a nondescript mid-century apartment building. The dog did not seem to be entirely house broken, though it was hard to be sure, and hard to blame the dog, as Caroline often left it alone there in the apartment for long periods of time. She did not spend much time at home. She subscribed to the daily *Star Tribune* and kept the hardwood floor in the otherwise empty second bedroom covered in layers of newspaper. The dog always seemed a little unhinged when we would finally on occasion take it down in the elevator, which was all stainless steel and equipped with spherical space age buttons with a little red light in the center of them that I liked to press. Once outside, the dog would bound clownishly around, bumping into parked cars and pedestrians and parking meters.

At this point Caroline and I had been spending time for quite a few months together. It was winter still, February, which is in Minnesota, no matter what you might have heard elsewhere, the cruelest month. She managed a sushi bar downtown and did not suffer bullshit. She never mentioned her boyfriend Geoffrey except when she was angry. Then she'd tell me how he was the only man who had ever really understood her. He was the only man who had ever really loved her. The English Sheepdog, apparently a purebred but without the benefit of papers, and a full-length fur coat, another gift, would then be cited as evidence of his love and understanding. I had never claimed to understand her. Her boyfriend Geoffrey had, in addition to the dog, also given her this fur coat, bona fide pricey mink or something. I never asked what it was, the exact species of pelt, though I preferred it to the dog, and her in it.

My uncle had once worked, before his last conviction, on a mink farm up north. He'd told me about it, the cages all in rows, the pervasive stench. After they skin the minks that are ready to be skinned, they grind up the resulting furless mink bodies and feed them to the other minks, those minks that are not yet ready to be skinned, I assume. The fur coat looked awfully good on her. I don't believe I ever told her so, and that's one of the things I regret. As a rule, I tended to keep my mouth shut in those days and let people think what they wanted to think.

Caroline was surprisingly small and lovely, a little what some might call Rubenesque. She was exceptional in this and in other ways with fine skin and long blunt cut blue-black hair. She liked to wear the fur coat over a little black cocktail dress, or on occasion over little or nothing at all. I tried to treat the coat as if it were just another coat, though I'd never seen anything quite like it, or like her. I tended to sport a motorcycle jacket in those days, a T-shirt advertising one obscure band or another, blue jeans, and underneath I wore, pretty much year-round, for comfort, a red union suit. We made an unusual pair. Polar opposites in most every regard. I suppose that was a good part of the attraction.

So it was February and Caroline told me, as I said, that she wanted to visit her boyfriend. She wanted me to drive her to Duluth in my Delta 88. Caroline did not own a car. She did not drive. She got around town by taxi when she needed to get around town. So she wanted me to drive her up to the prison and wait while she went in and had her visit with this Geoffrey whom I had never met. I wasn't quite sure how I felt about this. The federal pen in which Geoffrey was incarcerated was a hundred and fifty miles or so away. Was there a waiting room or would I have to wait in the parking lot? It was not sounding anything at all like my idea of a good time, hours driving a two-lane highway through desolate frozen farmland, a radio wasteland, in the rust bucket Olds with its feeble heater, snow blowing and drifting across the road, icy conditions and limited visibility, just to sit waiting in the cold while Caroline talked with this guy. And about what? I'd inherited the car from my uncle, and it had to this point been trustworthy. But I didn't want to push it too far.

Caroline kept after me, said she'd pay for gas and a hotel room, and though I was still ambivalent, I gave in and said all right. As the trip to Duluth approached, I began to wonder.

Should I be feeling jealous? Did I feel jealous? I thought maybe I did a little, but I realized I was also a little jazzed as well. It had been some years since I'd visited anyone in prison. My uncle was down in the state pen at Stillwater, but after about three years, we ran out of things to talk about, and I'd quit going to see him. Of course I wouldn't be going in and meeting Geoffrey in Duluth. Even if I wanted to, which I didn't, I wasn't on the approved list of people who could go inside and see him. I was content not to be on that list. I was content not to be on the radar at all, his or the Feds. I wasn't really involved in Geoffrey's business, other than being, I guess, involved with his girlfriend, who was, admittedly, conducting his business for him while he was locked up.

Caroline mostly took cabs but every week I'd drive her around to different apartments on the southside and wait in the Delta 88 or in a hallway or on a landing or sometimes in the apartment in the background or in the next room while she conducted business. I mostly just sat or stood silently, there but not really there, not really involved, though I could see how it might appear like I was involved, might appear like I was a lookout, or muscle, an accomplice even. But appearances can deceive. I'm not a big guy but not too small. I wrestled in high school. I played outside linebacker the last time South St. Paul won the state championship in football. The coach always said I had good instincts for the ball.

For the most part it was nothing, running these errands with Caroline. It didn't take long usually and then we'd go out to a club and party. The only time I'd get uneasy was when the Colombians were in town. They were the only ones who came to her apartment. Caroline would lock the dog in its bedroom. I would nod to the Colombians from the sofa when they came in. I'd stay there in the living room watching the television while they went with Caroline into the kitchen. It occurred to me once while the Colombians were there that I was probably the only guy in the apartment without a gun. I thought about how I might turn loose the dog if things went south, but I figured the dog would be useless. It would probably go after me. I would think about all the details I knew of Geoffrey's business, running down a list in my head. I would sometimes think, not seriously, just idle musing, about how much the DEA might like to know what I knew. Driving Caroline, I pretended not to pay attention, pretended not to care, but almost without trying I had compiled data. Timetables, addresses, names and nicknames, routines, scars and tattoos, distinguishing marks, quantities, secret stashes, a shooting gallery or two. I would think sometimes about what it would be like to drop a dime, about how I might bring it all down, and whether I could without somehow implicating Caroline, or me. But I figured I couldn't, and to what end, really?

So she would typically go into the kitchen with the Colombians for a while. At some point the clicking of the pilot light for the gas burner on the stove would signal that the transaction was more or less complete, and it was time to sample the goods. There were usually two or three Colombians. They were serious-looking dudes but sometimes I would hear them laughing and talking low with Caroline in the kitchen. My high school Spanish utterly failed me.

In these moments, Caroline in the kitchen laughing with the Colombians, I would wonder, should I be jealous? Caroline alone in the kitchen with these dangerous motherfuckers? I was sleeping with her, yes, but she was

Geoffrey's girlfriend after all. I was just the other guy. Was he jealous of me, up there in his cell in Duluth? Did he even know about me? I figured, yes, he must be jealous if he knows. But then why should I be feeling jealous here in the living room watching television? Caroline and I never did talk about it. She took care of business in the other room with the Colombians and I'd watch old movies on television, usually something in black and white, which I find less distracting than color, like *Seven Samurai*, until Caroline would emerge from the kitchen haze looking lovely, smiling, glassy-eyed, walking slowly toward me, a hip-rolling vision, bearing a propane torch and a loaded glass pipe just for me, like payment or a reward, though for what I was never quite sure.

I was working on the loading dock in those days, as I've said, a warehouse down by the river, a union job. I'd load cartons of books onto pallets and then onto trucks with a forklift all day. And there was the bartending gig a couple nights a week at McCready's Irish Pub, for kicks and a little pocket money. This was before it burned down. It was an Irish pub in name only, owned allegedly as a tax write-off by a seldom seen businessman named Ahlberg who had a towing business, the bar, a four-plex on the north side, and rumored other enterprises. There was never tape in the cash register. The bar manager, Ahlberg's girlfriend's sister, was afraid to be downtown after dark. She'd bolt for the suburbs before sunset and leave the place to the bartender, which several days a week would be me.

It was rumored that the Chinese mafia owned the building, which had long ago been a fire station with a stable out back. The alleged Chinese mafia upstairs of the bar would occasionally call down for a case of beer. I'd carry one up and leave it outside their door, swapping it for the envelope of money that would be waiting on the floor outside the locked wooden door. I assume it was locked. I never tried the door. Once or twice, I saw old Chinese men in long dark coats and hats like in movies from the fifties going up the back stairs with young women in short skirts. Caroline liked classier places and didn't much care for McCready's, but she began to stop by on the evenings when I worked, occasionally transacting business in the back room by the pool table.

*   *   *

When Geoffrey was paroled later that year, that's where I finally met him, in McCready's, though I didn't know it was Geoffrey at the time that I met him, a Sunday night in late autumn, long after Duluth, a typically slow night like Sunday nights tended to be, almost nobody in the place. Caroline and I were listening to the jukebox. I was at the far end of the bar. Caroline was sitting across from me.

I'd heard rumors that Geoffrey was out on parole and back in business but had not given it much thought. Caroline, as far as I knew, had not heard from him. We had not discussed him, his return to society, its ramifications for her, the business, or me. It was something I did not ask about. She seemed out of sorts, and I'd been keeping my mouth shut for the most part, waiting to see how it all played out, assuming that at some point something would happen.

So there we were, Caroline and I, sitting across from each other, not talking. A couple walked into the bar, a man and a woman looking like high rollers, stylishly dressed, unlike the usual clientele. The woman sat at the other end of the bar and the guy stood there and looked around, taking it all in like he might just buy the place on a whim. He had an air of confidence about him approaching smug. He finally slid onto the barstool next to the woman and I went down to wait on them.

He ordered top shelf whisky drinks for them both. The woman was tall, blonde, good looking, I guess. She was looking off elsewhere, already bored. She left on her coat. I dusted off the bottle and I poured a couple plenty strong like I always did. I set them up nicely on napkins, as if McCready's were a classy joint, which it was not. He slipped a hundred-dollar bill from a fat wallet that looked like alligator hide, or something likewise exotic or endangered. He tossed the hundred on the bar like it was nothing, and he looked at me. He was really looking at me. I held his gaze for a moment maybe. Then I glanced down the bar toward Caroline. She was studying the ice in the bottom of her glass. I picked up his money and took it to the register. I slipped the bill beneath the tray.

I brought him his change and he gathered up the pile of bills, tossed a couple back on the bar. I let them lay. He said something or other and we had some small talk, the weather, the Twins, whatever. Then, as if I were no longer there, he turned to the woman, who had not said a word. He nuzzled her neck. He might have kissed her. He might have whispered something in her ear. But I wasn't watching. I was making my way back down to the other end of the bar to where Caroline sat frozen, as if she had not moved since I'd left. After a while, after more whispering or nuzzling, the stylish couple tossed down their drinks and the man put on his coat. Caroline had still not moved or spoken. On his way out the door, the man looked back towards us, as if amused. He tipped his chin slightly with a hard little smile and went on out the door.

When I got back from clearing their glasses and picking up the tip, Caroline began laughing, a little too loudly, a little maniacally it seemed to me, and quite unlike Caroline as I had come to know her. She stood up abruptly and knocked over the barstool. She asked did I know who that was, the guy with the tall blonde and a taste for top shelf whisky. I had no clue and I said so. That was Geoffrey, she said. I felt all kinds of feelings. I tried to sort them out. I was glad I'd been clueless and therefore relaxed and cool in what could have potentially been an awkward situation. But why the small talk, and why no greeting for Caroline? And for whom had Geoffrey intended the cold parting grin?

After I closed up that night, after I closed out the till, pocketed the C-note, put the rest of the cash in the safe, after I locked the front door and turned out the overhead lights and came back out into the bar, I found Caroline standing beside the pool table looking small and faint in the dim neon light from the Grain Belt sign on the wall. I went over to her and embraced her. She scooted up with some endearing effort onto the pool table, her short black dress sliding up her legs.

To this day the aroma of stale beer and chalk-on-felt triggers in me a deep aching nostalgia and nothing's ever been quite the same. Thinking about it now, she may have already been pregnant when I finally met Geoffrey. In Duluth, we'd checked into the Best Western with an eight ball and a bottle of champagne. We had no luggage. We went straight to the room. I turned on the TV and popped the cork. We drank champagne from plastic cups and snorted cocaine off a Gideon's Bible in blue leatherette. At some point I went into the bathroom, and I looked at myself closely in the mirror. My heart was pounding wildly. There was a vague resemblance, but I was not immediately recognizable to myself. When I came out of the bathroom, Caroline was stretched out on the bed wearing nothing but the fur coat.

At that point I was glad I'd said all right, that I'd agreed to drive her to Duluth to see her boyfriend. I pulled my shirt over my head and shrugged half out of the union suit, the top of it hanging off behind me like my own red hide. In the motel light I could see that Caroline's coat was beginning to look a little rough, the fur matted in places and not so much elegant anymore, swerving toward roadkill. I shrugged off this line of thought and slowly opened the coat and gazed upon her and her amazing skin and her hair and all. For a good long while Duluth and Geoffrey and the rest of the world disappeared, and it was just the two of us and the fur coat.

Afterwards while still in bed she called Geoffrey at the prison to find out about visiting hours. I lay quietly there while she talked to him with the very same sweetness with which she'd spoken to me. We were unclothed, our legs still entangled. The TV was on with the sound turned down. And she was talking to him. I was lying on my back with my hands behind my head and not otherwise touching her while she talked to him. I gazed up at the water-stained ceiling. I could see nothing recognizable in the shapes. I'd heard that he stood her up before he went away, that is to say he spent his last weekend as a free man not with her but with a couple hookers and a pile of cocaine in a high-rise luxury suite. I tried to imagine Caroline that weekend alone in her apartment with the English Sheepdog. I tried to imagine her out on the town in her luxurious coat. What had she done that weekend while Geoffrey was having his going away party with the hookers? It seemed impolite then to ask. I guess I'll never know.

Caroline was still talking to him, and I was watching *The Big Sleep* with the sound down low. Lauren Bacall and everyone else it seemed was smoking and I badly wanted a cigarette too. But I didn't want to get up. I didn't want to move. I did not want to completely untangle quite yet. I was waiting for her to get off the phone. I was biding my time, I guess, waiting, without knowing it, for the final untangling, the long good-bye. It would all be over in a few months, Caroline and me, our fling, her condition, though I did not know any of this at the time. It seemed at the time, entwined at the Best Western, our bodies touching in places, our heartbeats, hers and mine, slowing inside our chests, Caroline curled in her sad fur coat talking on the phone, Geoffrey nearby in prison talking to her on the phone, the dog locked in the bedroom back in Caroline's apartment in the city waiting for her return, me shrugged half out of the union suit, intently watching Lauren Bacall smoking a cigarette, me craving a cigarette and pretending not to be listening to Caroline talking to Geoffrey in prison, and outside the window the leaden gray February sky blanketing all of Duluth, it seemed at the time that it all might in fact go on indefinitely. At that point I had yet to meet Geoffrey. At that point the future had been determined, though I couldn't yet quite see it from there. At that point I still might have imagined us together at some point. I might have imagined our child. I never imagined the way it would go down, Caroline leaving town right afterwards for California, telling me she hated my guts. I can't imagine now how else it could have gone down. At that point, though, I was just waiting for Caroline to get off the phone.

Laundry

Looking back, it maybe wasn't a great idea, fucking my next-door neighbor. You might prefer I call it making love, but my capacity for euphemism is presently low. Not actually my next-door neighbor, but a woman who resides in a one-bedroom two floors up in the Oak Grove Apartments. We first became acquainted in the laundry room. I haven't been down there now in weeks. I have bought new underwear and socks. Tonight, his car sits smugly again at the curb, her new boy. We passed once on the stairs. Hey, dude, he grinned, stupidly oblivious. I'm only the neighbor to him, some guy on the stairs. Hey, I said. What's up?

Roll Tide were her first words to me. A Saturday night, me starting a load of whites, nursing a domestic beer. Pardon me? I said. Tide detergent, she said, invented in Tuscaloosa, named for the Crimson Tide. I admit I was impressed. I remember her tipsy laugh and crooked nose, the warm hum of the dryer against my legs. She sat cross-legged on top of a coin-operated industrial washer. I don't recall what all else was said. A single bare light bulb hung from the ceiling, one hundred watts of brightness. The cozy smells of fabric softener and chlorine bleach. Just she and me and our respective dirty laundry, hers brimming with blue towels, blue jeans, and fashions. Delicate underthings peeked coyly from her basket here and there.

Our teeth clicked together on the first attempt, but we soon recovered, got it right, got into it, a kiss, both of us lit up with the breathless surprise of our unexpected lustfulness. My bag of quarters hit the floor and they scattered like a casino jackpot paying off. The machines worked steadily on our laundry beneath us. The smooth white porcelain steel felt fine. We sucked on each other's faces for quite a while. Our hands and limbs became involved.

When the spin cycle ended we broke apart for air, a deep breath, another look at each other. We shared the dregs of my warm beer. My lips tingled. We emptied, folded, started the next load. And started in again. Like I said, looking back now, it maybe wasn't a good idea. But at the time? Let me tell you.

It was Saturday night and everyone else in the world was out having fun, flashing toothy smiles like television ads for credit cards, pharmaceuticals, Japanese cars. She was twenty-four, on the rebound I later learned. I was thirty-three or so, divorced, half-heartedly wallowing in my vague angst, dwelling on such things as mortality and traffic tickets. Then, as I said, she walked in, Roll Tide, in shorts, hip concert tee, a glimpse of bare midriff. And then the kissing and the rest. As I've said.

Outside, it was autumn, bright leaves falling from trees in the park down the street, the remaining birds lazily chirping. Of course, it didn't last. Weeks blurred past, the usual heart-racing starry-eyed bliss, eating pizza or Chinese take-out on the floor of her apartment or mine, watching horror flicks and football. Up and down the stairwell every day. My legs became firm. Mostly we couldn't keep our hands and mouths off each other. Mostly we did things which, looking back, I can't say I regret in the least. Nevertheless.

My work began to suffer. I lost my focus. Bills went unpaid. Milk went bad. I missed a date in court and a warrant was issued. Laundry piled up in mounds. I began to rehearse a breakup speech: It's not you, it's me. You're too young, I'm not ready, and so on. But I was procrastinating.

And one cold late autumn day, after a Hitchcock matinee at a dingy little art theater, we returned to her apartment once more. She, my neighbor, my lover, more so than ever, it seemed. It was sublime. My old neckties, our glistening sweat. The headboard banged away like a marching band until the whole world dissolved in our frenzy. And then, as we lay there, unbound, spent, and dreamy, there in the glow of that pure moment she told me.

I could not comprehend at first. Vertigo. We can't, she said, no more. Of course, she continued, still friends, and all that. She recited my own speech, more or less, as I recall, verbatim. I felt as if I were falling from a great height. She was sorry. I couldn't breathe. I begged some, I'm ashamed to say, suddenly sure she wasn't too young, and I was, after all, ready.

She turned away and looked out the window at the bare trees. I had visions of Saturday nights alone in the laundry room, another guy's car parked outside. I pulled on my rumpled clothing and stumbled downstairs.

* * *

Days and nights have passed, weeks of them, much as I'd foreseen. And now I face another Saturday night. The rest of the world et cetera et cetera. I wear the last of the clean new socks and boxers, my favorite jeans, a 1987 World Series sweatshirt. I open the window and take a breath. There's a hint of spring and snowmelt in the air. A robin, maybe the first of the year, flies by in a northwesterly direction, toward the park down the street. And it occurs to me. The park side laundromat three blocks down. I can almost hear the deep hum of the commercial dryers, the talk show static on the dusty television bolted to the wall above the bulletin board of lost cats, band flyers, and roommates wanted.

I see myself walking home, my laundry clean and folded. I don't look up at her window, at the shadows dancing on her wall. I ignore his car gleaming in the streetlight. This is a good idea, I think. A shower and a night of sleep. I'll wake in the morning refreshed, put on clean clothes and go off to work a new man.

So I gather my laundry into a sack, a pocketful of change, *The Sporting News* special spring training issue, and I head down the street with my head held high. Someday I will look back on all this, I think. And if I happen to see her, my old neighbor, on the stairs, or in the laundry room, I'll smile and say, hey, and I'll mean it. Yes. Someday soon, I'll simply look back.

Postal

My grandfather worked at the post office for thirty years. He took us to Tiger Stadium. It is illegal to send ammunition, flammable liquids, and illicit drugs through the mail. My father wrote memos to us on birthdays and other occasions. I had my mail held as soon as I heard the news. I hitchhiked to my grandfather's funeral. It seemed like autumn, but it could have been February. My last ride was with a gambler on his way to a high-stakes poker game in Chicago. I had hoped for a girl. Bicycles are a communist plot, the gambler told me. His Torino overheated outside Ypsilanti. My uncle is a reluctant stamp collector and drinks alone. I suspect my mail carrier sometimes neglects his duties, perhaps spending the afternoon fishing or sitting in a tavern. Opening mail is always a gamble. The gun on the wall is a literal gun. Watch where you point it. The gambler dropped me at the station where I bought postcards and a ticket for the train. I associate the postal service with Lucky Strikes, bowling, big band music, gun shows. My grandfather drove Buicks. Automobile accidents are not, I scrawled on a postcard. Destruction has an aesthetic. Consider the syntax of entropy and the singular pattern of shattered glass. I did not send it, lacking a stamp. My grandfather was a fan of the popular crooners before the war. Tonight, my neck stiffens. My damaged car leaks fluids in the impound lot. Somewhere people light votive candles and pray. I consider traffic patterns as a metaphor for health. Streets are arteries, cars corpuscles, collisions are something else. Somewhere people dance and play. My troubled relationship with narcotics resurfaces at the hospital. The painkillers deliver me down a dark hallway. I trail I.V.s from my arm screaming that I am one of the Kennedys. Nurses play tie the boy down. A little girl crawls under the altar. A little girl flies through the windshield. A train leaves the station. Never the same train twice. The gun show returns to a billboard beside the church. We roamed Tiger Stadium swinging souvenir bats like nightsticks. Five to one odds against. Trees grow in the streets of downtown Detroit. My grandmother hit my brother with a rolling pin. He threatened to kill us all. The importance of a good utility fielder cannot be underestimated, my grandfather once told me. Or was it the gambler? My grandmother complains that no one ever calls. Mail still arrives addressed to my dead grandfather. My grandfather told me of a young widower calling on the widow of a pilot. She readied herself for their date. He smoked a cigarette and waited on the sofa. Eighty-seven percent of all mail carriers have been attacked by dogs. Her poodle pissed on his shoe. My father hid the guns. I hoped for a girl. My brother hitchhiked to California. My grandfather married the young widow. He and the poodle grew old together, hating each other. After the funeral, I hugged my grandmother. I took the train home to the gun under the mattress, the painkillers, the unopened mail, a little girl still flying, and all these postcards.

Rhinelander

Grimsrud and I returned home from The Corner Bar expecting to find as usual only the individual quarts of milk and partial loaves of white bread, this month's block of government cheese, case of ramen noodles, and dregs of a liter of Canadian whiskey. It was therefore initially high excitement for us to discover a bona fide fugitive occupying the old floral sofa in the living room, making himself right at home upon it. Our other roommate, Sikorski, was visibly wrought while introducing us to the fugitive McNulty. Sikorski was actually physically shaking as he made the introductions. I took note of this. Sikorski had always been an icon of cool, our big city roommate. An icon of cool until McNulty's arrival.

Home was what we called this clapboard house in the student ghetto at the edge of the downtown strip, conveniently in walking distance to the bars and the Food Mart. The old frame house had been partitioned into student apartments with little apparent thought or planning, and likely in violation of local building codes and whatnot. Home then was where the fugitive McNulty had commenced to lay his head, to make himself at home, that is. My room, which opened onto the living room, had once been a formal dining room, to judge by the fancy cut-glass ceiling fixture and the built-in buffet. The other bedrooms upstairs included one, Sikorski's, that had once been a walk-in closet, a low-ceilinged dormer with a drafty window and no heat register.

In the living room, McNulty had been laying his head on our sofa, on a gallon-size Ziploc freezer bag of weed, sleeping there, so to speak, if you want to call it sleep, his head on this big bag of weed there on our sofa, eyes almost but not quite closed. As if any of us would dare to touch McNulty's bag of weed. Or his sinister greasy backpack, which slumped between the sofa and the big green upholstered chair that I discovered last summer outside the Goodwill drop box in the parking lot at the end of the block and carried back home down the alley balanced on my head. There were three of us roommates, a number that had dwindled from seven due to summer when some of those of us enrolled at the local college leave town. I and Grimsrud and Sikorski remained, working at jobs within walking distance to pay tuition in the fall. Grimsrud at the second-run movie theater, Sikorski the old folks' home, and the plastic injection factory for me. Historically, it was late in the era of affordable higher public education, a decade past the summer of love, early in the war on drugs. Ronald Reagan, a B-movie cowboy actor, had been elected governor of the great state of California.

The days passed uneasily. When he was there at the house McNulty stretched out on the sofa, occasionally with his eyes closed, but in two weeks he had yet to take off his boots. He otherwise made himself at home. He played our records without cleaning them and would leave them spinning on the turntable, the needle nodding insistently against the label at the vinyl's end. When he would leave the house, he'd holler without variation and regardless of who was home or the time of day or night that should any of us punks touch his shit we would die.

The word was that McNulty's unexpected relocation to western Wisconsin was due to a disagreement with the Twin

Cities chapter of the Bandoleros Motorcycle Club regarding payment for a quantity of crystal meth and a two-pound bag of weed. There was also apparently further bad blood between the parties. He may have also kicked the shit out of one or more of the bikers. We gathered innuendo and allusion. We learned things secondhand, from Sikorski in an uncharacteristically hushed voice when McNulty happened to leave the room for a moment, and piecemeal clues from McNulty himself.

McNulty was not especially tall, but he was noticeably wide. He took up a lot of space, physically and psychologically. He was bulky and menacing in an unsubtle way. We learned interesting details of McNulty over the days and the weeks following his appearance in our living room. McNulty had been in prison as well as in many jails. McNulty hated cops and had beat up a cop or two on occasion. He likewise had been beaten plenty by cops, to hear him tell it, here and there over the years.

McNulty's mother was from a reservation in North Dakota, Sikorski told us. I figured his father must have been Irish. We heard McNulty had been on the street or locked up since he was eleven or twelve. It was a heart-aching story, but I found it difficult to muster sympathy for little McNulty while big McNulty was eating our ramen noodles and drinking our milk and had essentially occupied our living room, regularly threatening our well-being. I found myself feeling a little guilty though for having had a house, such as it was, and my own drunken father around throughout my own unremarkable mid-American youth.

McNulty had been in more jails than I had been in states, though I had dreams of someday crossing the Mississippi River, of seeing mountains and the big sky country. I had been in a couple different states, including Florida once, the Sunshine State, which is another story. McNulty told us of a time he was in jail in Palm Beach County. He did three hundred push-ups and three hundred sit-ups every day and would brawl alongside the Mexicans against the blacks in great awful battles. I had never brawled, never been in jail, and had never been to Texas, where McNulty punched a deputy sheriff in the face. He spent some time in Texas.

So McNulty came to be laying low in our living room in America's Dairyland unbeknownst to anyone except us roommates. We could thank Sikorski for McNulty's presence. Sikorski knew McNulty from their childhood on the mean streets of Northeast Minneapolis. Also, there apparently was a handgun in McNulty's backpack, which he liked to keep close at hand.

It occurred to me that the smart thing would be to just leave town until this all played out or blew over. But there was an undeniable allure, as well as inertia at play. I felt as if I could not leave or look away, even when, and it seemed certain they would, angry bikers arrived to kick down the door. They would be looking for vengeance, looking for blood. For meth and weed and money. They'd be looking for McNulty, though most likely they would not be terribly discriminating. Anyone in proximity who was not McNulty would be nonetheless at risk. Is it in Ecclesiastes where it says about the wise man and the fool, that they both will die like dogs? I was hoping to be at work or otherwise elsewhere if and when it all came to pass. I considered myself neither wise nor a fool, and I began to think more seriously on going west. If only I had the means to go west.

I was without a car in those days. We were college students of varying degrees of seriousness ranging from not very to not at all. Sikorski appeared to be the most serious, though it could have just been nerves. He suffered from anxiety when he was away from the working-class inner-city neighborhood of his youth. He remained on constant alert, spooked by rural landscapes and our small college town. In retrospect, perhaps rightfully so. Sikorski wrote songs and poems, and his major was undeclared. Grimsrud was a business major from St. Paul, an ex-hockey player who played guitar. I'm from Rhinelander and was majoring in history, though I cannot remember why. They all called me Rhinelander, though I'd sworn not to return to the place, to my father's bait and tackle shop, where he waited smugly for my return, my failure.

I was attempting to teach myself the bass on a secondhand Fender I acquired from Arno, a former housemate, whom I'd heard still lived around town in a retired bread truck. Arno gave me my first lessons on the bass before moving out suddenly the previous summer. There had been artistic differences in the house as well as disagreements concerning the contents of the refrigerator. I tried to mediate but Grimsrud was adamant that we go forward without Arno in favor of a paying roommate, and this was when Sikorski moved in. We were also lacking a drummer and had been looking for one that summer so we could start a band called Rhinelander, which we all agreed, though some grudgingly, sounded better than Grimsrud or Sikorski.

McNulty occasionally would disappear into the bathroom, our only bathroom, at the top of the stairs, or wander into the kitchen to eat whatever he pleased of our food from the meager cupboards and the old fridge in which we had each labeled our quarts of milk and blocks of government cheese and tubs of margarine and bags of lunchmeat and white bread. McNulty ate our groceries and we said nothing.

Sikorski had been seeing a cashier at the Food Mart down the street, a long brown-haired girl with a lazy eye who, when she checked him out, slipped most of his groceries into the bag unchecked so he ate well on not much money. Grimsrud and I ate not so well on not much money, and even less so after McNulty. Sikorski's cashier drove an old VW bus, a relic from the summer of love and had, according to Sikorski, what she'd described to him as an oral fixation. We were awed almost to disbelief by this, and jealous of the groceries. But with McNulty in the house, our preoccupation with him took precedence over even sex and food. Sikorski could not sleep. He confided in me that he'd encouraged the cashier to stay clear of our house.

Trust was a rare commodity in our home in those days. McNulty did not trust us, even though we were all scared shitless. Sikorski did not trust McNulty, though he was like a stepbrother or second cousin to him and from the same neighborhood. Sikorski likely did not entirely trust his cashier around McNulty. Grimsrud and I had confided to each other remarkably similar fantasies featuring the cashier, and with McNulty's ongoing presence in the house, Sikorski seemed to be diminishing, coming apart in a way that inspired a glimmer of hope for us in regard to the cashier. I did not trust Grimsrud in this regard. Honestly, I suppose I trusted none of them. I hid the money I earned working the early shift at the plastic injection molding plant that summer inside my bass guitar case, gradually accruing a full semester's tuition and then some.

We'd more or less lived in our living room before McNulty, drinking Canadian Club and sour, smoking weed and rocking out in naïve bliss. Grimsrud's big Marantz stereophonic receiver and turntable and floor-standing loudspeakers occupied one wall. The television did not pull in much chan-nel-wise, an unwieldy console unit from another decade inherited by someone or just abandoned by previous tenants. We mostly kept it on for fuzzy, green-tinged background visuals with the sound off in favor of the superior wattage and high fidelity of the stereo and the glory of our collec-tive collection of vinyl. And that, it gradually became clear, offered an unexpected point of reference, a serendipitous confluence with McNulty.

Someone once said, I believe I heard, that music soothes the savage beasts and similarly, we came to notice that McNulty dug music. He dug our music. He dug it like we dug it, that is, deeply and with a reverence beyond words. And so after the first couple awkward and sleepless weeks a shift occurred, and there were lulls of relative calm in our living room when he or one of us would drop the needle onto a record of McNulty's choosing. He'd occasionally emit what sounded like a reluctant grunt of approval when, while flipping through our crates of albums, would happen upon some bootleg Stones, or Charley Patton or Furry Lewis and "Shake 'Em On Down." McNulty would on those occa-sions wordlessly pass around big joints he rolled from his big bag of weed and though the undercurrent of physical violence and menace did not entirely go away, it sunk a little beneath the surface as we carefully smoked without speaking. I wondered if I was the only one who felt this, but I kept my mouth shut about it.

McNulty loved the blues. This should not have been a surprise, I suppose. Sometimes in the evening when we gathered the courage to return home and slunk exhausted back into our own house, McNulty would holler at us as we tried to slip off to our rooms without his notice. He'd holler at us to join him in the living room. And so we'd enter through the beaded curtain into what had once been our living room and what we all had come to silently consider McNulty's room. One of our records would be playing loud, louder even than we played our records, which was loud. His big bag of weed lay there upon the coffee table, open and spilling onto the cafeteria tray on which we'd cleaned our own meager nickel and dime bags in the halcyon days before McNulty. McNulty's bag was comically huge and magical. It never seemed diminished no matter how much he, and we, smoked from it. No wonder the Bandoleros wanted it back.

McNulty rolled great thick joints using several rolling papers licked together, deftly twisted in his scarred and meaty hands. His hands resembled train cars, battered and dented and heavy with cargo. And to our cautious glee, he could be almost generous in those moments, like a gruff and homicidal older brother. We spent hours then sitting in the living room, as we once had before, smoking and listening to the blues and sometimes reggae, not saying much if anything at all, maybe watching the shadowy figures on the silent television while the joint made its sacred journey around the room.

McNulty, it turned out, played the harp. He played it damn well, something of a surprise, beautiful, soulful sounds emanating from an angry mass of tattooed scar tissue. He carried a harmonica in his back pocket and sometimes pulled it out to play along with a recording or by himself the blues like we had never quite heard them, live and authentic. And I, in spite of my fear of McNulty, could not help but picture him and his harp onstage with Rhinelander, the band. Me, Sikorski, Grimsrud, and McNulty playing bona fide hard-earned blues, with a drummer to be named later righteously backing us up. I imagined adoring women in the crowd, Sikorski's cashier among them. But McNulty's contempt for us seemed so unambiguous and absolute I didn't quite know how to pitch the idea to him.

* * *

One afternoon Grimsrud and I and Sikorski were availing ourselves of twenty-five cent drafts at the Corner Bar, postponing our return home. Sikorski was looking more frazzled than ever, mumbling that we had to get rid of McNulty before the start of fall semester. The Food Mart cashier was there, a pretty girl with the long brown hair and the lazy eye. Sikorski announced suddenly that he had to get out of there, that he was hitchhiking back to Minneapolis. The bar was fairly crowded, and we were fairly buzzed, having gathered the courage to nick a small amount of weed that morning while McNulty was upstairs in our bathroom. The Bandolero's weed was potent stuff and the scene in the Corner Bar verged on sensory overload. Sikorski indeed left. Grimsrud and I remained. We looked around in amazement.

The Food Mart cashier looked over at us. At least it seemed as though she did. She's keeping us guessing, I remember thinking. Grimsrud said she's looking at one of us, most likely me, meaning him. I, ever the pessimist, said she wasn't likely looking at him or at either of us for that matter, but if on the unlikely chance she were, she'd most likely be looking at me and not Grimsrud. You couldn't be sure what she was looking at, and that was part of the charm. She might appear to be looking at you and smiling but her one eye would be gazing off apparently at some other person or thing and there would be that sliver of doubt that perhaps the other person or thing was the rightful recipient of her lovely smile and attention.

In the midst of our speculation, she walked over and slipped up to the bar between us. We were speechless. She started talking and told us her name, which was Lisa, and that she was through with Sikorski, who had no interest in travel or adventure, she said, which were things for which she lived. Sikorski is provincial, she told us. Even though he'd said once he'd go with her to Colorado it had become clear to her that he was not going to leave Northeast Minneapolis. Lisa told us she'd been working at the Food Mart to save up to move to Boulder where there was a Beat school of poetry, Allen Ginsburg himself, and summer jobs to be had at the national park. She told us she was packed and ready to go. Sikorski, we learned, had backed out at the last minute, perhaps due to the distraction of McNulty, but she was going regardless. I had only ever seen her at the Food Mart in her cashier's outfit, and once or twice disappearing into the twilight of Sikorski's closet. Here in the neon and cigarette haze of the Corner Bar, on the verge of leaving town, she appeared more beautiful than ever. She wore carpenter's pants and a *Blues for Allah* concert tee. Of course, the Bandolero's weed likely factored in.

Suddenly I heard myself talking, more than I'd talked since McNulty came to town. I heard myself telling of my Montana dreams, my yearning for mountains and big, big sky. Things I'd never before said aloud to anyone. Grimsrud looked at me skeptically and snorted, miffed and disbelieving. Lisa though was listening to me with a curious look in her eye.

I was about to say more when McNulty appeared in the door. The vibe in the bar changed like a switch had been thrown, a current of menace making a circuit. He shouldered past the bouncer and the crowd parted as he walked up to the bar. The bartender quickly placed a beer in front of him. I did not even see him order it. McNulty drained half the glass and wiped his mouth on the back of his hand. He turned then, ignoring me and Grimsrud, and gave Lisa a leer. Then he said something to her, a remark so foul I repressed it completely. I could not repeat it now with a gun to my head. A thought came faintly through the fog in my head like a voice from a faraway radio. This is it, time to go, I think is what it said. But I could not move. Unlike Grimsrud who slid off his barstool and sidled over to the jukebox where he fed it quarters and punched buttons.

When the Sex Pistols started blaring from the speakers, McNulty finished his beer and said loudly to no one and to all, Fuck punk rock! I'll show you punk rock! He bit off a chunk of his beer glass with a loud crack. He was looking at Lisa, and looked to be grinning, beginning to chew on the broken glass. Sid Vicious was singing "My Way." It was hard to tell if McNulty was grinning or grimacing, but he was grinding the glass down pretty good from the look of it. I guess you'd want to if you were going to swallow it, which seemed to be where this was going.

At that point I saw Grimsrud, who had made his way to the front of the bar, slip out the door. I tried to tell myself that I was still standing there because I wasn't a coward like Grimsrud, because I was standing my ground, that I wasn't afraid, was just biding my time. But I knew that was not the case. I was just too fucking high to move my feet one in front of the other. I watched as the bouncer approached our end of the bar. I recognized him from a house party where the football team had amused themselves by smashing all of the glassware and most of the furniture. An offensive tackle, I think he was. It was our house.

The lineman put his meaty paw on McNulty's shoulder and started to say something tough and clever when our houseguest reached up and grabbed his hand. He bent it back hard at the wrist and the big man's knees folded. McNulty punched him quickly twice in the face. Another football player rushed over. McNulty let the lineman drop to the floor and turned in a fighter's stance, his big fists up and ready, his grin glittering in the bar light. The brawl had begun.

I still could not move, until Lisa put her hand on my arm, leaned into me and whispered, let's get out of here. The hairs stood up on the back of my neck at those five words, the warmth of her breath in my ear, her leaning up against me. I felt an electrical charge, startled awake, and followed dazed behind her through the crowd. I followed her out the back door, which closed behind us like a vacuum.

It was quiet outside. I looked up at a sliver of evening sky that glowed above the alley. I looked at the few dim stars and was filled with the knowledge that we were all just hurtling through space together on this planet. Then Lisa took my hand and led me toward her van. As we walked hand in hand, I heard a low rumbling in the distance like a swarm of angry bees. Or, I realized a moment later, like motorcycles, big V-twins with open pipes maybe, southbound on Highway 35 it sounded like, somewhere north of town.

* * *

Lisa parked across the street from the house and waited for me in the van. I went in the back door. The house was empty. I threw some clothes in a duffel bag, and my paperback copy of *On the Road*. I grabbed my guitar in its beat-up case and the little Pignose practice amp. Then I ducked into the living room for one last look around.

The rumbling was deafening as I reached the van. I climbed in and was sitting shotgun when McNulty came hurtling down the sidewalk past us toward the house. I heard a sound like a screen door being torn off its hinges. The rumbling was approaching a roar and my stomach tightened into a fist. I felt momentary concern for McNulty, though I couldn't quite bring myself to wish him well. I'd left his backpack for him there between the sofa and the old green chair.

From the passenger seat, it felt as if all around us things were moving, some receding, some growing closer, some circling and circling around us. I recalled hearing somewhere that the Badlands are lovely and strange. Lisa started up the van and shoved a tape in the cassette deck. The music began and we were rolling slowly down the street when headlights appeared. A horde of motorcycles, an unwashed crescendo of chrome flashing light, leather and denim and noise approached and washed over and past us to engulf the old house that I called home, into the driveway and up onto the lawn.

They spilled into the yard like a Viking war party as Lisa wheeled the van around the corner, turned up the volume, and drove toward the interstate. We passed the Food Mart where I saw an old bread truck parked in the back of the lot, outside the glow of the mercury vapor security lights. I said a silent good-bye and good luck to good old Arno. As we rolled out of town I said more good-byes, to Sikorski and Grimsrud. To the time clock at the plastics factory, to The Corner Bar, The Food Mart, the old clapboard house, to home. Good-bye to McNulty. Good-bye, perhaps, to Rhinelander.

I wedged my duffel between the seat and the window, leaned back and looked at the beams of the headlights reaching out northwesterly into the darkness. Lisa was drumming her fingers on the steering wheel and when I glanced over, she was looking at the road ahead, smiling in the dim light of the dashboard. The music was strange, unfamiliar to me, a strong backbeat, funky and bluesy, but not really funk and not quite the blues. It sounded all right, I thought, it sounds damn good. I rested my head on the duffel bag and took a deep breath. I savored the sweet smell of the Bandolero's weed, blending perhaps with the government cheese. I closed my eyes as Lisa aimed the van westwardly. I felt further from the old clapboard house already, ready, I believed, for wherever might come next.

Memphis

I was between jobs, getting by on what I'd skimmed from the till at my last bartending gig. I liked to sip Stoli straight up to keep an even keel in the wee hours and they fired me for drinking on the job. So I was biding my time at a roadhouse by the river, nursing a longneck, tapping my foot to a rock-a-billy trio with a stand-up bass when there, I swear, across the smoky room, appears the girl of my dreams.

She was sporting denim shorts a half size too small, halter-top of a style that took me way back. Eyes dark and shadowed, lips curling into the semblance of a smile. I thought she looked like trouble. I made a beeline through the crowd. Up close she looked even better; a pug nose once broken that had healed off kilter. A gap between her front teeth begging me to worry it with my tongue.

We danced hard, bumping hips with bad intent. When finally the band unplugged, and the lights came up tattooed bouncers herded me and Sheila out into the night. Of course I didn't know then that Sheila was not her real name.

We necked in the gravel parking lot straddling my bike, a chromed Virago, beneath a fat harvest moon. Indian summer. Sheila's back arched back over the fuel tank as if for a fashion photo shoot. Blue lights flashed over the scene. A two-way radio crackled nearby, but we were bulletproof. We rode away when we were good and ready, a projectile flying through the barrel of the night.

We spent days together, a week of them, maybe, Sheila apparently also between jobs. We never got around to discussing careers. Aquamarine 320-thread-count sheets draped the king-sized waterbed in her basement efficiency. She kept a hot wax machine. We went at each other with abandon, improvising with what was at hand—thrift store neckties, ice cubes, a roach clip, the wax, and the like.

We lived on smoothies, loading all manner of fruit into the blender, powders from the health food store and pricey vodka. Mostly we were fucking or sleeping, night and day, practicing epilation, reciting aloud favorite passages from my dogeared *Captain Maximus*. Motorcycles turned her on, she confessed. I taught her how to lean into the corners, to exit rolling on the throttle. When the rent came past due, I cashed my last unemployment check.

The next morning, I awoke to a rumble. Sheila it seemed had lifted my keys and wallet. I pulled on my jeans, stumbling outside barefoot just in time to see her riding south with the wind in her hair in the general direction of Memphis. An awfully beautiful thing to behold. I dropped to my knees in the street. Sheila! I cried. Goddamn. I still long to wrap my hands once more around that lovely throat. Even now I think, if I'd known then what I know now, I'm afraid I'd do it all pretty much the same.

Vulcan

Chance sweats and squints into the lighter fluid fumes wavering above the fifty-five-gallon burn barrel in his shadeless yard in Bessemer on a Sunday in August. He's backed his truck up to the barrel, an Early American bedroom suite piled into the bed. Tire tracks in the dying lawn lead from the open patio door at the back of the house. He strikes a match, and the barrel erupts with a concussion. A ball of orange flame engulfs a box of paperback romance novels and a selection of lacy underthings.

He stumbles back, a little stunned, his eyebrows singed. He drains a can of beer and picks up a photo album, spilling snapshots of the two of them: young lovers canoeing the Cahaba River, tailgating before the Alabama-Auburn game, newlyweds at sunset, her head on his shoulder, and Lois scowling beneath the statue of Vulcan at the park on Red Mountain. Chance had always liked the big iron monument, the homely god with his bare ass, hammer, and torch high over Birmingham. Lois called it a civic embarrassment. Driving home with his bride on their wedding night, Chance had seen the light shining from Vulcan's torch turn from green to red, signaling a traffic fatality somewhere in the metro area. He'd said nothing to Lois, unable to put into words the thrill he felt.

Chance puts the photo album on the tailgate. He feeds the flames five years' worth of crafts he made in the garage while listening to the Braves games on summer evenings. A footstool, napkin holder, a curio wall shelf, candlesticks that have never seen a candle. He eases into a lawn chair and opens another beer. He is not yet drunk, in his mind only slaking a deep thirst. He sweats all the time these days, addicted to painkillers since the accident at the steel mill, and the surgery that left two discs in his back fused together. He's been working for a high school buddy, framing houses, but he has trouble keeping up with the rest of the crew. Lois has taken to telling Chance that this marriage is no longer working either.

Lois is gone again, to an all-day revival, she said. She left this morning in her best dress, a little black number she got in Atlanta. She left with a pineapple upside-down cake like she used to make for him. She said she'd pray for him. She said not to wait up.

Chance spent the morning emptying the house of everything that reminded him of Lois. Not much remains inside. His vinyl recliner. A miniature Statue of Liberty. The rented TV. A framed photo of Bear Bryant. Chance gets up to add to the conflagration from the great pile of household goods and clothing in his truck. He contemplates a redwood cribbage board. They'd taken his new truck out to California on their honeymoon. She'd sulked all through the Alcatraz tour. Driving through a giant tree, they'd argued, something stupid about ecology. He'd joked that trees make good stumps. The cribbage board sends sparks into the air.

As Chance nears the end of the twelve-pack, he grows impatient, and his mind becomes clear. He feeds the flames a shoebox of letters. He was stationed out west at Fort Carson when they got engaged and she'd written to him every week. Now the letters seem like a cruel joke. He's feeling righteous, ready to turn up the heat. He climbs into the truck and pushes the sofa off the tailgate. He feels a pop in his lower back, drops to one knee and groans. Flames lick the sofa where it has landed against the barrel.

Coins fall from beneath the cushions. The heat is so intense he can only watch them shine brightly out of reach in the lawn. Sparks smolder and ignite in an upholstered armchair still on the truck. The Midnight Blue paint begins to blister on the tailgate and rear quarter panel. He stares as the taillights sag and drip in fiery clumps, giving off a toxic black smoke. The photo album bursts into flame like a magic trick.

The garden hose lies in the grass, but the fire has grown too big. The truck is now involved. It is a fire to be reckoned with. Chance climbs clumsily out of the truck bed. He stumbles backward into his neighbor's yard where he takes refuge behind a statue of the Virgin Mary enshrined in an upended and half-buried cast iron bathtub. Lois had been a virgin when they first met. Or so she'd claimed. Anything seems possible now.

The truck came equipped with dual fuel tanks, which makes for two impressive explosions that occur in rapid succession. Chance slumps against the bathtub shrine. He wonders if perhaps he has made a mistake. He imagines Vulcan, lonely, overlooking the city from his great pedestal, and he wonders what color his torch burns tonight.

O Happy Living Things

The Volvo sedan is an ugly car, yes, but it is Bender's and paid for and he is mindful of where he parks it in these days in New Orleans. It has been sideswiped twice in the new year while legally parked. No note left beneath the windshield wiper like in the civilized times of old. Rear-ended twice. Someone keyed a long scratch along the street-side quarter panels and doors. He suspected his neighbor, Webb, a surly widower, a retired security guard who still flashed his cheap badge and cussed out most people who crossed his path. They'd exchanged unpleasantries when Bender and his wife moved into the neighborhood, and he parked the U-Haul in front of the old guy's house. Sherry said they just got off on the wrong foot, but Bender argued there was no right foot with Webb.

And now, almost a year to the day that Sherry left him and the city, after receiving notice this morning that his rent is doubling to reflect the shortage of housing in the unflooded neighborhoods, while merging onto DeGaulle, punching through radio stations looking for something more angry and raw than the usual trad jazz and swamp pop, neither of which is synching with his present state of mind, an Explorer in front of him inexplicably stops for a yield sign and Bender's Volvo thuds into it. The woman seems frightened when she gets out, as if she thinks he might have hit her intentionally. Lately there have been rumors of such things: insurance scams, carjackings, simple assaults.

He unfolds himself from the car and stands beside it, a lanky unshaven man with a slight beer belly in a ratty Black Sabbath T-shirt and jeans, blinking in the merciless sun of early summer. Dirt darkens his fingernails and the creases in his hands. He wears paint-spattered work boots and is aware that he might not look as harmless as he feels. He gives himself a start these days when he happens to catch a glimpse of himself in a mirror behind a bar or in the reflection of a storefront window. He looks like the ghost of his grandfather, a sullen sharecropper who was given to long periods of silence punctuated by unpredictable and vicious rants, a man who, family legend had it, beat a mule to death with an ax handle.

The woman gives him and then her bumper a quick look. She looks at the looming vacant concrete gulag of the Fisher housing projects across the street, jumps into her car, and speeds off without a word. Which is fine with Bender, who does not relish the idea of waiting for the cops. He has other things to do for the next four or five hours of his life and has lost too many days already in the labyrinth of parish traffic court. He has clients to see, people whose lives and troubles help Bender to feel in comparison slightly less fucked up himself. There is work to do on the house, which seems pointless these days but is still his preferred method of procrastination. As long as the cars still drive and nobody's bleeding or unconscious the best thing to do here is to shake hands and drive away. Or just drive away.

In the months before Sherry left, he had begun to see the Volvo as a physical manifestation of his emotional state. The taillights worked sporadically, shorting out in the rain.

The car exhibited collision damage on all quarters, the front bumper wired to the chassis with perforated metal strapping. And one lovely Saturday in April, after hearing that old man Webb had been shot in the back of the head while walking home from the corner store, Bender removed all the emblems and badges and chrome from the car and repainted it himself with a case of flat black spray paint. He was not particularly upset about Webb's death, he noted, though he was disconcerted by the crime's proximity. Many of his clients lost family members to violent crime and, looking on the bright side, he decided that this experience might help him be a more effective counselor. Sherry though was upset by the murder and decided that a dead neighbor was the last straw.

* * *

The Fourth of July Bender calls his pal Guidry to say he's ready to break out the SKS, a cheap Chinese-made assault rifle he picked up on a whim at a Baton Rouge gun show shortly after Sherry moved to Atlanta. Sherry had worked with Guidry's wife at the community college, and after the divorces the two men had begun meeting at the Oasis, a bar near Bender's house where they played pool and talked about how much they enjoyed being single again.

Guidry tells him that his Accord was stolen from outside his home some time over the weekend and recovered stripped of its engine and burned on a desolate stretch of road in the east near the abandoned amusement park. Bender says he'll drive.

The Volvo arrives in front of Guidry's cottage at dusk. Guidry emerges from the shadows of the porch and walks out to the car. He is heavyset with a blond crew cut and black plastic eyeglasses, a slightly bloated Clark Kent in chinos and a Hawaiian shirt featuring hula dancers and surf boards. They drive in silence through the darkened streets of Algiers, past boarded-up houses, decapitated streetlamp posts, and hand-painted street signs nailed to telephone poles. They drive to the levee where Bender parks the car in a vacant lot next to an abandoned pickup with out-of-state plates. The truck bed is spilling over with moldering sheet-rock and two-by-fours festered with nails, broken plumbing fixtures, asbestos roof tiles, and black garbage bags swollen like summer suicides dragged from the river. The hood and doors are gone, and a steel fencepost is embedded in the shattered windshield. An orange city citation pasted on the back window has faded almost white and is curling off.

They toss their empties into the cab of the truck and grab the box of cold ones from the cooler in the trunk. Bender gets the SKS, which he's cleverly hidden in a powder blue king-size pillowcase, and they walk across the empty street to the levee and climb the grassy slope. The fireworks display begins, the gaudy explosives firing from two barges moored across the river, dark shapes beneath the flickering skyline. A year out from the disaster and the place is overrun by carpetbagging contractors, con artists, crack dealers, and other such entrepreneurs, and with a per capita murder rate to rival Medellin and Baghdad. But it's been nobody he knows, besides Webb, whom he didn't really know or like. Nobody close to him. This is still, he tells himself yet again, a better place to live than Houston or Atlanta. What other place has this kind of soul?

But some days Bender is not quite convinced. Neither any longer is Guidry, a recently divorced architect with a backlog of rebuilding projects that are dead in the water due to the red tape down at city hall, but he is a native and deeply rooted to this place. Bender is a mental health counselor at a local nonprofit, so business is booming. The city is a laboratory for post-traumatic stress syndrome. Divorce, suicide, domestic abuse, and substance abuse are through the roof in this brave new world. He listens empathetically and encourages his clients to find outlets for their anxieties. Yoga, jogging, writing poetry. Guidry mentioned once in passing that discharging firearms can be remarkably therapeutic, and Bender has decided it's worth a shot. Professional research.

They walk up the levee and look around. Nobody in sight. They stumble down to the trash-strewn batture, flailing through the mutant brush. Plastic grocery bags flutter madly like flags of surrender in the leafless branches of anemic little trees. The explosions from the city's fireworks echo off the levee and they can see them through the brush and scrub trees. All throughout the city, the tiny sporadic pop and crack of black-market fireworks and gunshots. It's rained on and off and on all day and low, gloomy clouds hang over the city and reflect the garish fireworks.

Bender slides the SKS out of the pillowcase. He fumbles with it. Guidry sets down his beer, takes the rifle, loads it, and chambers a round. Guidry spent three years in the military before going back to school. Operation Desert Storm.

"Go ahead," says Bender. Guidry points the rifle in the direction of a grounded barge whose hull looms darkly in the brush at the river's edge. He fires three rounds, the reports loud and sharp and exhilarating. He hands the rifle to Bender and retrieves his beer.

"Happiness," he says, handing the warm gun to Bender who takes the gun carefully in an attempt to disguise his inexperience with firearms.

"First time I've seen you smile in months," Bender says. He means since the flood. He figures they have twenty to thirty minutes at least before NOPD shows up. If they show up at all. Not Our Problem, Dude. The National Guard is still patrolling the city, but they're most all across the river and in the east. Guidry paces back and forth behind Bender, drinking rapidly and chucking the empty cans into the batture.

The stock is blonde wood, roughly finished, crude, cheap, mass produced. Bender nuzzles it to his cheek. He sights along the short, dull barrel into the night sky to the east. He waits, and with the next round of fireworks, squeezes off half a dozen shots in quick succession. The adrenaline rush is instantaneous and sweet.

The neighborhoods in the east are still mostly depopulated. Of course, there's an outside chance a falling bullet out there might find some scumbag tearing out copper pipes and wires from a flooded house or stealing new appliances from a house being rebuilt. Or just as likely it could kill some hapless citizen walking home through the ravaged neighborhood. Bender adjusts his line of fire down toward the river, toward the rusted hulks of the abandoned barges. Falling bullets have always been something of a hazard here on New Year's and Independence Day, coming down on those days.

Once, while looking for the source of a roof leak, he'd found a neat round hole in the asbestos tile on the roof above the living room, from some new year long come and gone, from another place and time. The water stain had grown slowly on the ceiling like the map of an ancient world. The dark insistence of it had troubled Sherry, and him to some degree as well. Now a simple roof leak seemed benign and almost charming.

They hand the rifle back and forth in the rockets' red glare and manage to finish the box of shells just in time for the grand finale. The dueling barges let loose with a good five-minute barrage and they hot-footed back over the levee with the SKS warm in its pillowcase and a huge cloud of technicolor gunsmoke drifting slowly downriver towards them.

Back at the car Bender stows the rifle in the trunk and turns back to watch the last of the fireworks flashing and reflecting off the strange clouds and the smoke while Guidry sits impatiently in the car. Bender's ears are still ringing from the SKS, and there are sirens in the distance in every direction it seems. The downtown skyline has taken on a peculiar glow in the smoke and the haze, a cinder burning itself out in the mud beside the river. This city will surely be gone in a hundred years, thinks Bender. Quite possibly long before that.

*   *   *

They cross the river bridge and Bender drives fast through town, back streets, windows down, stereo blaring, through smoking intersections littered with the carcasses of spent Roman candles and black cats, silver salutes and plastic phantom missile bases. They careen down narrow potholed streets where cars are parked on both sides of the street and facing both directions, up on curbs and sidewalks. Sporadic pops and whistling bottle rockets report and echo as they pass. Could be fireworks or gunshots. Bender sprays the old Volvo through a flooded street where a broken water main has been gurgling good crescent city clear for the past two weeks. The car fishtails, bottoms out hard in a deep water-filled sinkhole but plows on through.

Bender takes a corner fast and out of the corner of his eye sees a dark shape lunge from between two parked cars. A dog, feral maybe. They roam the streets in packs, sunken yellow eyes, mange-covered ribs. There's no time to brake and no room to swerve, a narrow street lined with parked cars, and the Volvo slams into the dog with a sickening thud that reverberates from the bumper to Bender's hands on the steering wheel.

"Fuck!" he says, and by the time he looks up into the rearview they are half a block away and the dog is only a dark motionless shape in the street, receding into darkness.

"There was a dog…" Guidry says contemplatively, as if he were beginning to tell a story.

Bender drives on. He squints into the rearview mirror but sees nothing. The dog must be dead, he thinks, and there's nothing we can do if it's not.

"Oh happy, living things," he mutters, the line surfacing from some dark place in the past. In his mind he sees someone kneeling beside the dog, heartsick. He shakes the image from his head and takes the next corner, and the next, driving fast and without signaling, as if he is being followed and is trying to lose his pursuer. He and Sherry rescued a stray one Halloween and nursed it to health. A chocolate lab mix. She took the dog with her when she evacuated to Atlanta before the storm, and then again when she left for good. Bender believes that the end of his marriage began when he insisted on staying through the storm to watch the house. Their neighborhood did not flood, though for several days after there was no power, no communication with the outside world, no police or fire protection, only unbearable heat and fear and silence but for occasional gunfire.

"I have done a hellish thing," Bender says. In the days after the flood before the National Guard arrived, before power was restored, he holed up in the camelback of his house with a case of wine and some of Sherry's books. Sheets of half-inch plywood screwed over the windows. Inside, dark as a tomb. He passed the sweltering days and nights sleeping fitfully, drinking warm beer and wine, and reading her Coleridge and DeQuincy by flashlight until finally the alcohol was gone and the batteries all were dead.

"Blood has been spilled," Bender says to Guidry. He is calculating a rough algebra of velocity, blood alcohol, chance, and guilt. And in the end, it equals what's done is done. The next step in the equation is further. Guidry looks out the window deep in his own stream of consciousness. In a recent news conference, the police chief responded to a question about the spike in violent crime by saying this has always been a violent place, maybe it's something in the water. The kid who shot Webb was fourteen. The kid confessed. Said the old man wouldn't give it up, had told him to get lost, and turned to walk away.

Bender slows the car as they approach an intersection, looks both ways as they roll through the stop sign. He checks the rearview. He drives on, more slowly now through the gauntlet of rash heaps, flooded cars, rotting refrigerators at the curb, the thump and buzz of distant speakers, the occasional staggering pedestrian, lights flickering behind windows and from streetlamps. They ease past bars and storefronts with no discernible commerce and park in front of a tattoo parlor, a bright window beneath a precarious balcony.

Guidry walks inside the small shop and begins flipping through books of flash. Bender watches from the sidewalk as if at the aquarium. Nearby people are abusing musical instruments, transforming considerable rage into a mutant strain of rhythm and blues. He nods his head in time. He looks at his watch. Forty-five minutes to get uptown before the music starts. Trey's Denali opens for Morning 40 Federation. He wants a bar stool, room for an elbow and a bottle, a view of the stage. He goes in after Guidry who is still perusing flash.

"You sure about this?"

"I've been sure for years." Guidry is mumbling, beginning to fade, a faraway look in his bloodshot eyes. The tattoo artist watches them with slight disinterest from a stool, his burly colorful arms crossed. His face is riddled with an assortment of metal studs and rods and hoops.

"How long will it take to tattoo this guy?" Bender says, grabbing the book from Guidry. He finds the right page. He scans it quickly and jabs his index finger at a design. "This one here." It's simple, yet elegant. Timeless. Just the thing for an architect.

"Wife says I get a tattoo she'll leave me," Guidry mutters.

"Ex-wife," Bender says. "She's already gone." He looks out the window. Three roofers in ball caps, dirty jeans, T-shirts, and work boots stagger past, high on meth, passing around a tallboy in a paper bag, in search of Bourbon or some other kind of dull pedestrian trouble. A woman in a black skirt and white shirt emerges from a bar across the street. You do not see many women out in the city these days. The roofers holler crude suggestions at her. She flips them off and goes back inside the bar. They skirt the Volvo without incident, still bent on foul bravado. Bender watches them out of sight.

"This mean you're staying?" Bender says. The tattoo gun begins to hum. The artist hunches over Guidry, the gun buzzing beneath the bright florescent lights.

"Or else a memento," says Guidry. Bender watches the blur of the needle, the blood beading up on Guidry's forearm and thinks of clever things to say but cannot muster the energy to say them. He walks back out to the waiting area where he drops onto a filthy legless sofa.

He flips through big glossy magazines from another place and time, but his mind cannot focus to read, and the photos and colors seem mocking and unreal. Bender tosses the magazines and walks outside. In the bar next door he orders a beer to go and stands outside drinking from the big plastic cup. The sky looks strange above the ruined city, but the beer is cold and good, and soon uptown the band will begin to play. He drains the beer and goes back to check on Guidry.

*   *   *

The artist finishes and the gun buzzes to a stop. He pulls off the rubber gloves. He snaps a digital photo.

"Looks great, let's hit the road," Bender says as the artist applies a gauze pad. The bar uptown will be filling up and he conjures his favorite perch, a stool near the end of the bar with a passable view of the stage, convenient to the john, the narrow hall that leads to the courtyard. An infamous dead local poet looks down in mild amusement from a framed black-and-white photo fastened to the wall with drywall screws.

When they step outside, the young woman in the black skirt is leaning against the Volvo. She's drunk, Bender notes, though these days that's like remarking upon the fact that she has shoes on her feet. Or that she has feet. Although she does not, in fact, have shoes on her feet. They are lovely feet, shapely and luminescent on the littered concrete, and Bender pauses to admire them. She is a gregarious drunk. Her hair is dark, her lips are red, and her eyes are moist.

Bender looks at her and inhales deeply and tastes the residual tang of gunpowder that hangs in the air. Guidry stands in the neon glow of the tattoo parlor window and looks up into the sky as if he were an ancient sailor charting his course by the stars. The woman leans back on the flat black hood of the Volvo, crucified by the stars. She is holding her shoes, cruel-looking things with thin straps and dangerous heels. The sky has turned almost green, and if Bender weren't in a hurry to get across town, he would linger and savor this moment of beauty and grace in the face of the impending disaster that is without a doubt looming somewhere in the near future. But he is in a hurry.

"I hate to disturb such a lovely scene, but we have someplace to be," says Bender. The woman turns her head and appraises him.

"Where?

"Uptown." He nods at her footwear. "Those are some cruel-looking shoes. Would you like a ride?"

*   *   *

Her name, she says, is Maria. She sits between Guidry and Bender as the Volvo hurtles uptown. Bender feels the warmth of her thigh against his leg, and he is unable to think. He wonders if Guidry is feeling it too, simple human contact. He feels as if he might weep. There is a moment, the feel of her leg and the air through the open window, which adds to his buzz and equals a desire to continue driving and never stop. But the car hits a pothole. Maria is thrown laughing toward Guidry, and the moment passes.

Now that the fireworks are over and families are safe at home in front of their televisions, the city streets turn dark and menacing. Statistically the odds are very good that every other asshole on the road is drunk or armed or both. Big trucks with tinted windows, ladder racks, and out-of-state plates roar through stop signs, straddle the centerline, and fly against traffic down one-way streets. Since repainting the Volvo, Bender has been less inclined to yield, maintaining a hard course just inside his lane, daring them to cross the path of this battered Scandinavian warhorse so clearly and terribly far from home. They rock inside the rudderless Viking warship as it navigates the toxic waters of the lower Mississippi.

Maria asks do they want to get high. Bender declines—class A narcotics are no longer part of his program, but Guidry replies in the affirmative. He's full of surprises tonight. She produces a small quantity of white powder in a folded paper bindle. She and Guidry take turns snorting off a key. Bender watches discreetly, his pulse quickening while he negotiates the rain-slick streets. Is that the key to Guidry's Civic, Bender wonders? To his old house? It seems poignant, metaphorical in some way Bender can't quite grasp. He wants to ask but he doesn't. He sniffles reflexively, savors vicariously a little imaginary metallic postnasal drip, the old heart race bumping along. He unconsciously accelerates down the street. Professionally speaking, Bender cannot condone self-medication but, off the record, he finds it is often quite effective.

*   *   *

They are making good time keeping to the backstreets when suddenly he turns a corner to find an armored personnel carrier blocking the street, doors flung open and blue lights flashing. Bender slams on the brakes. The tires lock up and the car skids to a halt throwing Maria and Guidry into the dash. Two young soldiers in combat fatigues look back and glare at them for a moment before turning away. A small crowd has gathered on the sidewalk and in the street around a dark mound on the pavement. Beyond it, as if dropped in from a Victorian novel, several men are struggling to push an open carriage backward down the street and off to one side. A couple seated on the high upholstered seat hold each other, heads together as if in prayer, no doubt wishing they'd opted for Vegas. Guidry and Maria get out of the car and walk toward the scene.

Bender reluctantly gets out and follows them. They work their way through the ragged murmuring crowd that has trickled out from a nearby corner bar. The military vehicle's lights illuminate something mysterious in the street. Bender's mind struggles to identify the glistening object, confused and nostalgic at the earthy smell and the incongruity and cannot at first recognize what appears to be a large animal slumped against a parked car, its legs splayed out.

"A horse?" he says.

"Mule," says Guidry.

"Dead?" Maria holds her hand over her mouth and gapes at the mule, whose head lolls to one side, its huge body heaving, its eyes shining in the man-made light.

"Heart attack." An old woman in the crowd gathers a nylon windbreaker around her thin shoulders and puts her hand on Bender's arm. She looks up at him. He pats her hand, then turns away.

The crowd breaks up and shuffles away and Bender can smell stale beer and smoke drifting from the low-ceilinged bar, the faint rusty scent of blood on pavement. Maria kicks the door of a parked car. She's maybe crying. Down the street the flashing lights of a tow truck making its way the wrong way up the one-way street play off the wet brick and weathered clapboard of the silent shuttered houses.

Bender looks back at the dead mule. He feels as if he is floating somewhere above the scene, watching himself and wondering at the fact that he seems to feel nothing for this dead animal. He can almost taste the decay, the hundreds of years of past lives that thicken the air here.

"Let's go," Guidry says. "The second line starts here."

Guidry puts an arm around Maria who leans into him, and they weave back to the Volvo. Bender aims the Volvo uptown and the three of them are back in motion, moving again over the broken streets and past the broken buildings, the darkened windows and doorways. They are silent, the radio down so low it's as if it is coming from another galaxy, only the rumor of a broadcast, spectral jazz whispering. The only other sounds are the sounds of the mechanical workings of the Volvo engine, transmission, brakes and shocks, and the hush of the balding tires on the wet pavement.

* * *

Bender turns at the riverbend and follows the levee to where traffic lights hang darkly over an intersection. He slows, looking both ways and rolls on through and is momentarily blinded by high beams and off-road roll-bar halogens from a block away, a four-wheel drive truck, late model, lift kit, mudders, speeding toward them down the narrow street. He could pull aside or stop, but he doesn't. He has a sense of things building to a crisis, a moment to take a stand. He holds steady and at the last minute the truck swerves to avoid hitting them full on and there is the awful screeching of metal on metal. The Volvo's side mirror snaps and slaps against the door as the two vehicles pass so close they can smell the cigarette smoke drifting from the truck's cab with a few bars of clear channel country music. The mirror explodes and is gone, showering the inside of the car with broken glass. Bender slams on the brakes. He looks in the rearview. The truck has stopped down the block.

There are two guys, one of them in a cowboy hat, glaring at a scrape along the side of their truck. The Volvo's side mirror lies between them in the street. Bender knows that nothing good can come of any kind of conversation with these guys. He doesn't foresee a handshake on this one. But running away doesn't seem right. And to where? He realizes the passenger door is open and the car is empty. There's Guidry standing beside the car, stretching as if just awakening from a nap. And Maria is walking around the back of the car. She stops in the middle of the street.

"Hey, dumbfucks!" she calls out to the cowboys. She is standing barefoot with one hip out, a cigarette in her hand. She points it at them. "People live here, you know." She is a sight there in the streetlight, barefoot and looking all at once tough and frail. Bender just watches and thinks, it's just another car wreck.

The cowboys spit in the street and start toward them in a malevolent drunken stagger that might be funny in another situation, one in which Bender was clearly an observer rather than participant. Maria stands her ground. Bender watches her, transfixed, his head hanging out the window. He is reluctant to relinquish the wheel, to venture out from the battlewagon into the night. He tries to consider his options, but his brain is responding slowly. Then he hears Guidry's voice.

"Pop the trunk." Bender's hand obeys, reaching out to push the trunk release. The trunk opens softly behind him.

By the time Bender opens the car door and steps out into the street, Guidry has the pillowcase out of the trunk. He unsheathes the SKS from it as he strides past Maria toward the contractors. When they see him their eyes get wide. Guidry pulls back the slide and it snaps into place with a serious metallic click. Before Bender can fully assess the situation—the odds that these guys are armed, the fact that the SKS is out of ammunition, the distance to the bar—the cowboys are falling all over themselves getting back to and into their truck.

The truck roars off, extension ladders clattering like a mouthful of loose teeth. They stand in the empty street for a moment, Guidry, the empty rifle, Maria, and Bender. They should feel victorious, but it feels oddly like another loss.

* * *

Bender parks the Volvo discreetly around the corner behind a gutted elementary school, easing alongside a dumpster overflowing with desks, chairs, blackboards, and exercise equipment. The streetlight has been fortuitously shot out, providing this end of the block with a nice shadowy gloom. Guidry is silent, pensive even. Bender senses that Guidry's spirits have lifted in the wake of the encounter with the roofers. He is feeling a lift from the adrenaline himself, and they walk to where a crowd spills from a funky building onto the sidewalk and into the street, the low thumping of amplified bass and drums pulsing through the thick night air such that they can feel it in their chests.

* * *

They stand in the back at the bar. There is a good crowd and the band already playing. The three of them are feeling the warm bond that comes from staring into the abyss together, Maria sandwiched sweetly between Guidry and Bender. She is wearing her shoes and has gained stature in Bender's eyes. There is nothing to say, so they drink and nod to the music that washes over them like a wave.

After the first set, Bender ducks out for fresh air and a smoke. He starts walking back to the car, a small bad feeling pulling him along. When he reaches the Volvo, he sees that the windshield has been shattered by a cinderblock that rests on the front seat in a sparkling pile of shattered safety glass. The tires are all slashed, the windows and headlights and taillights broken. He doesn't need to get an estimate to know it will cost more than the car's worth to get it back on the road. The glove box hangs open like a drunkard's mouth, its contents strewn across the front seat. He finds the registration and insurance card and pockets them. He walks to the back of the car. The trunk has been pried open. He sees the blue pillowcase empty on the ground, and he goes cold.

What's one more gun loose in this town, he thinks. An image of Webb dead in the street is followed by a wave of nausea. He rummages in the trunk for a screwdriver and removes the license plate. He pries off the VIN with the screwdriver and pockets the thin piece of stamped metal. The light is bleeding into the sky downriver, and the darkness is fading again into dawn. A dog barks and a rooster crows.

Bender stands back and looks at the wreck. "There was a car," he says, but nothing more. It is already gone, already past, and he can no longer summon elegy or invocation for moments such as this. He turns and walks away. A block from the bar he stoops to pitch the license plate beneath a blighted house and continues on his way.

The band is back onstage, and Bender orders a beer. He rolls the cold, wet bottle across his forehead. Guidry peels back the gauze pad to show Maria his new tattoo.

"Cool," says Maria. "I've got one of those." She turns around and lifts her shirt. There, just above the waist of her skirt, centered on her lovely spine, brightly colored in purple, gold, and green, a little fleur-de-lis. Bender feels a jolt of surprise and disappointment when he realizes that his friends have paired off.

"I've been thinking," Bender says. He's thinking about Sherry, her garden now overgrown with weeds, about Webb, the old man's dark and empty house. Bender and Webb had disliked each other at first sight and never exchanged more than a word or two, but the old man had always lit up around Sherry, tipping his hat, talking about their gardens. He gave her Creole tomatoes and Sherry would give him bell peppers and limes.

"You gonna get one too?" says Maria. She turns back around and leans into Guidry whose hand falls easily onto her hip.

"Nah," Bender says. He looks up at the dead poet on the wall who gazes sadly back at him. Bender recalls a line from a film he saw in his youth: the more you drive the less you think, and he quotes it aloud. They look at him, puzzled, glowing in their fresh lust. Bender raises his bottle, toasts them, and drinks. "You two get a cab? I'm going."

* * *

Bender walks down the middle of the street, vaguely in the direction of home, away from the abandoned Volvo, away from the music, his friends. The streets are empty, the houses are dark. The fireworks have diminished to occasional illicit pops and the cruel birds of early morning have begun to mock him with their cheerful announcement of a brand-new day. But it is not a new day. It is still the same day, always the same day these days, a long, cold, gray dawn of the soul. Bender turns the corner looking down, lost in his thoughts, watching his feet to navigate the fractured sidewalk and he doesn't see the three black kids sauntering toward him until it's too late to turn and run.

He quickly scans the street, heart pumping the old fight-or-flight. Nobody else in sight. He continues walking slowly toward them as if unconcerned. They meet in front of a boarded-up shotgun house with spray-painted orange hieroglyphs on its century-old shiplap siding echoed by scrap two-by-fours nailed across weathered louvered cypress shutters in haphazard X's. Bender and the kids size each other up. A chance meeting of nomads in a post-apocalyptic wasteland. They are just boys, small, not even teenagers, dressed in oversized white t-shirts and baggy jeans. Trick or treat, Bender thinks. He has about twenty bucks in his wallet. If they have a gun, he'll drop it and back away, hope they let him run.

"You got ten bucks?" the tallest one asks. It doesn't sound like a question. He's holding his shorts up with one hand at his crotch.

"We trying to stay off drugs," says a skinny kid wearing a new-looking Yankees cap sideways. Chances are the kid has never been out of Orleans Parish let alone to the Big Apple. He has a nasty scar across his cheek that wreaks havoc with what would otherwise be a disarming smile. The third kid just glares at him with a pure and ancient hatred.

"What?" Bender says. He's trying to decipher the words, the logic. Why ten bucks? Why not five? Or twenty? And how.... These boys are stoned out of their minds, eyes red and watery, and Bender puzzles for a moment on the logic of how ten bucks might help them resist the temptation to get high. His brain can't make the connection and he gives up and almost laughs.

"Why you wanna do that?" he slurs. He realizes he sounds like a ridiculous old white guy trying to sound hip or like he's mocking the kid's dialect, but he doesn't really care.

"Stay off drugs?" Bender straightens himself up as best he can. "Why would you want to do that?"

"Give it up, motherfucker!" yells the third kid in the shrill voice of an angry child. The city is full of these kids. Sherry thought she could save them when they first moved here, but ten years in the Parish school system left her defeated and hopeless. Bender, with his years of training and experience, a degree and a license to practice, knows he should have something to say to them, but he's got nothing to say and nothing he's willing to give.

"Sorry, boys." Bender dismisses them with a wave and walks on past them and unsteadily down the street. He feels their eyes on his back, his neck prickling. He can't tell if they're following him or not, but he does not look back. He walks on, trying not to think about, but thinking about Webb. He wonders if the old man tasted this brand of fear. He wonders if he heard the shot that killed him. He wonders if the tomatoes are still growing in Webb's backyard, thinks maybe he should check on them. One of the reasons, only one of the reasons, that Sherry left him and this city was that she did not feel safe here, and for that he did not blame her. He can hear her voice saying, you can die here if you want to, but I will not.

His feet feel like concrete blocks, but he wills them to move forward, concentrating on lifting them one at a time in sequence, like running in a dream. And just when he thinks he may be all right, something whirs past his head and he is falling. The pavement rushes up hard and he slams into it. He curls up, instinctively hands over his head. There is the sharp crash of breaking glass nearby. Only pain and sounds. A bottle smashing in the street. Laughter, curses, the sound of running footsteps. A dog barks somewhere and then he hears a strangely familiar sound. A bird is singing. He cannot remember the last time he heard a bird singing.

He gets up slowly, his heart pounding as if it will explode, and he looks around. The street is empty once more in the cruel light of dawn. I'm alive, Bender wonders. A haggard rooster high-steps into the street from behind a parked car, its head up defiantly. A misshapen hen and a brood of dirty yellow chicks appear behind him. Bender stops and watches her worry them across the tarmac, through the broken glass and into overgrown weeds between two vacant shotgun houses while the rooster perches on a fence like a vane. Bender silently wishes them well. He hopes Guidry and Maria are safely necking in a cab on their way to his place or hers. He stumbles down the broken sidewalk. The best thing to do is to just drive away, but the car that brought him here no longer runs.

There's a lighter shade of gray in the eastern sky when he finally turns the corner onto his block. He walks down the middle of the street between the facing rows of modest shotgun houses, some freshly painted and some still boarded, others like Bender's somewhere in between. He's been working on it for months but from the street it still looks in decline. He's exhausted and exhilarated too. He does not go to his house but crosses the street. He makes his way down the narrow alley alongside Webb's house, a place he's never been. He looks back from the narrow alley at his house, Webb's view of his sorry place. There's the porch where Sherry liked to sit and read with an iced coffee or a glass of wine.

In the back yard he looks over Webb's garden, Creole tomato vines struggling up through waist high weeds and fallen trellises, tomatoes on the vine, tomatoes fallen and rotting into the pungent soil. The only tool a gardener needs here is a machete. He scrounges three ripe tomatoes from the tangle and sits on Webb's back steps.

Bender thinks about the Volvo and the assault rifle. They are gone and he lets go of them. He's gotten pretty good at this. He looks out over the neglected garden. Maybe he'll come back when he's slept and clean it up. Pull the weeds, water the plants. The Sewerage and Water Board turned off Webb's water, but Bender can fill a five-gallon bucket at his house. He'll pick the tomatoes, bring some to Guidry, who he knows likes a vine-ripe tomato and mayo sandwich. There's a good chance Guidry will be at the Oasis tonight, maybe Maria will be there too. Maybe they'll all walk down to the levee and look up at the moon and the stars flickering dimly above the wide river and the doomed old city. Or maybe they'll drive further south down to Grand Isle to the end of the world and look out at the lights on the offshore oilrigs glittering like stars over the Gulf. That's as far as he can see right now. He wipes a tomato gently on his shirt and bites into the thick flesh as if it were an apple. Warm, sweet juice runs down his chin and his mouth comes alive with the taste of it. It's the best damn tomato he's ever tasted in his life.

Summertime

Summertime, the little girl on the levee sang, a small husky whisper too sorry to be sexy, lost in the wind and the boat horns, in the thick summer air. She sat cross-legged looking off nowhere, mumbling to no one in particular a sad story of stranded in New Orleans with no gas money to get home sweet home to Ohio, Iowa, or wherever. A few off-season tourists might stop and listen, throw her some bills or change. She told them she was living in her car, but I knew she stayed in a squat off Rampart, a shotgun opening onto the sidewalk. I followed her there one night from a bar in the Marigny where she was laughing and shooting pool with other kids like herself, pierced and tattooed, defiant, young, and flush with quarters and dollar bills from her gig on the levee. I just sat at the bar, cold gin and tonic sliding into my veins, sweat beading on my temples, my back, under my arms, running down my face and body like small cool fingers.

*   *   *

Summertime in this city the air gets thick and comes alive, wraps itself around every lost soul here. They stay indoors or move from one shady doorway to the next like lizards, blinking. At night when the hazy sun has burned itself out, they come out into the dark heat and move slowly as if they're underwater, below the levee and the rippling surface of the great unseen river snaking its deep way around us silent but for the occasional lonesome foghorn. The girl worked the tourists most days, the crack of noon til three or so, then moved from the levee to a shaded step beneath a balcony off the square. I know. I walked the Quarter learning how to make myself invisible, fading into the heavy air, molecule by molecule until I was a seersucker ghost, a white blur wrinkling the air as I passed by. But she could always see me, first a glimmer of recognition after weeks of nothing, not a look but an involuntary twitch, a hesitation in the deep beat of the bongo she wrapped her legs around, an awkward pause in Gershwin's lyrics that changed each time she sang them. I kept my distance, watched from behind dark glasses, sideways glanced as I glided by, still becoming invisible, fading with the faint strains of her awful voice, nowhere near Joplin but her mournful story pierced me even as I saw its lie.

* * *

Summertime, the ghosts appear in the haze down the street, always turning the corner when I draw near, and at night in the blue glow between the streetlights, wavering and dancing, unwilling to leave this decadence. Nights like these the world closes in, and the streets become crowded. I am glad to be invisible. One night like this the girl with the drum between her legs and the awful ragged-throated voice packed up her sad act and walked downriver, disappeared into the strange shadows on Governor Nicholls. I followed a block behind her as if in a trance, until she disappeared. Deep faraway sounds like drumbeats, a pulse of breath and sharp words drifted toward me. I made my way to the place where she'd disappeared, a narrow alley. Her drum lay where it had come to rest on the cobblestones against a battered downspout. I heard footsteps and they echoed in my head like a heartbeat. I smelled something like fear and sex rising above the constant earthy funk. At the end of the alley a man in the shadows loomed, a small figure crouching beneath him. I tried to call out but could not summon a voice. I stooped to pick up an empty bottle by the neck. I broke it against the flagstones. The figure turned at the sound of shattering glass and ran. The girl sat where she'd pulled herself back against the wall, into the shadow, a bare leg, a shoulder, a scraped and bleeding elbow all glowed faintly in a light that came from nowhere. From the shadow her eyes appeared and I became visible in their light. I dropped the broken bottleneck and walked towards her. I knelt beside her.

* * *

Summertime, the river gives up the bodies, ripe and bloated, bobbing along the shore, drifting slowly past the docks, the moored barges, the overgrown batture of the Bywater. A body decomposes in forty-eight hours in the summertime river they say. I watched once unseen in a murmuring crowd as uniformed men pulled from the river the body of a man in a white linen suit who had jumped from the Algiers ferry. He was wearing only one shoe, his one bare foot wrinkled and pale. The white coat and his shirt were pulled up over his head and face, his round belly exposed like an obscene moon. The men lifted him by his arms and legs and laid him onto a heavy black plastic bag and zipped it up. They loaded the black cocoon into a white truck, its lights flashing red and blue across the silent, sliding river.

* * *

Summertime, my loneliness grows heavy and settles onto me like a shroud. The girl in the shadows in the alley was the pale white of the man from the river, her belly a small sphere, exposed and pierced with a blue metal ring that I longed to feel between my teeth. I knelt beside her and placed my hand there, felt her warmth, sweat, blood, the small rising and falling between us. She made sounds, small sounds from her throat, like an old song heard through a door, muffled, unclear, her own sad lyrics. I could only stare. I felt a great emptiness then, and a tear slid down my weathered cheek. We did not speak the same language, and her lies I realized all be true. I carried her to the nearest street corner and flagged a cab. I lifted her into the back seat, gave the cabbie the address on Rampart Street and a twenty-dollar bill. His radio was playing something familiar and sentimental, a song I once knew. I watched the taillights fade like red eyes into the fog, and she was gone.

* * *

Summertime lasts forever here. But then suddenly it's over and the world is visible again, edges again defined, the air light and subtle. The solstice brings cool air, and the sky regains its color. As the streets grow crowded with the tourists, I stay more and more in my small room, up a narrow tilting stair, the tall windows open, the ceiling fan turning slowly a rhythmic grind, becoming hypnotic with each groaning revolution. I close my eyes and dream about the girl, the heartbeat she beats on the drum clenched tight between her legs, the hoarse cry of her voice, her painful try to conjure up a dead woman's song. She is gone now I know. Iowa, Ohio, or wherever. Or perhaps gone for good, but I can still sense her here, a smell that thickens in my mouth in the heat, a taste of summertime, the big hush of the river, our funk and our decay.

* * *

Summertime fades further into memory as I make my way to the river. I dress in my best suit, my dark glasses, the elegance of countless summers past. Tonight I throw money to each mime, each busker, each young lost soul with an outstretched hand. When I reach the landing, my pockets are empty. I wait in the shadows, apart from the chattering crowd, watch the ferry approach over the dark river. And as I board the ferry, I hear her voice rise up from somewhere neither near nor far, and she is singing awfully, summertime, and I can taste the moment metallic and right.

Engaged to Death

She did not share my fascination with secondhand shops and flea markets. It was summer in New Orleans. Her favorite book was Bataille's *Erotism*. We passed a junk store on Airline Boulevard on our way to the airport. I dropped her off for her flight and stopped at the junk shop on the way home. The man inside looked me over. I should tell you that I wore my hair short in those days. I was dressed in a black T-shirt, jeans, and boots. I can guess what you do for a living, he said. I'm quite good at it. I did not know how to respond to this. Here, he said. I'll write it down on this piece of paper. He wrote something on an expired page from a daily desk calendar. When you're ready to leave, you look and tell me if I'm right, he said. I browsed the store. Though I was tempted by the battered plaster statue of some unidentified saint, I walked finally to the counter empty-handed. The man turned over the calendar page and slid it across the counter to me. Written on the back in a child-like scrawl were the words: engaged in death. The poem started there, took shape in the obsessive syllabic form in which I was writing in those days, lifted from Berryman's *Dream Songs*. I'd been torturing syntax and abusing the line. I'd done away with punctuation. I told the junk man he was wrong about me, but immediately I felt unsure. I left feeling like a mortician with amnesia. I went home and read the book by Bataille, wrote things in the margins. I wish I had kept that piece of paper. I realize now that this is not the poem and that he might perhaps have been right after all.

Sunshine, Park Bench

I recall once in another world meeting my wife for coffee at a kiosk near a crosswalk. We strolled through the British Petroleum Bio-Environmental Sciences Quadrangle sipping our beverages in humid silence. A café au lait for her, and a small medium-roast shade-grown fair-trade Guatemalan for me. We were flirting with financial ruin and drinking too much in those days. On that at least we agreed. Alcohol, that is, but coffee too. We were hungover in the wake of a couple bottles of an earthy red from Argentina the previous night. I blamed the sulfites. On top of that a little jittery from too much caffeine, and yet we were having one more coffee to get through the afternoon and home for the first drink of the evening.

We found an unoccupied bench beneath a sprawling live oak and lowered ourselves onto it. A remembered line, Samuel Beckett I guessed, flickered almost into coherence, something about sunshine and a park bench. But it slipped away from me. I sighed heavily.

"What's with the heavy sigh?" she said.

"What?" I said, sounding more defensive than I'd intended. I glanced at her surreptitiously from behind my sunglasses to see if she intended to pursue this. I've always been a firm believer in choosing your battles, and this was not one I was choosing. She looked out across the dying grass of the quad, a look of deep discontent upon her face.

I tried to truly see her as she was in that moment, a fairly attractive woman who'd suddenly found herself in her late thirties and was none too happy about it, married to a man she sees, perhaps not incorrectly, as depressed, not so attractive anymore, and none too happy about either. Though not entirely unhappy, but that might have been wishful thinking. And of course, she wanted to have a baby for some reason, which was incomprehensible to me back then. We'd been having sex like clockwork oranges, the bedside table strewn with pungent herbal teas, thermometers and fertility books, a voodoo candle and whatnot, all to no avail. There was bad medicine in the air back then, in the water, all around us. I felt we were swimming in it.

Students strolled by oblivious, I imagined, to this older couple who looked to them, if they noticed us at all, no doubt like someone's wasted parents, perhaps their own. Each of them carried a handheld cellular device on which they tracked the intimate details of their lives. They wore variously styled and colored earpieces and I idly wondered what they were listening to, or if the devices were only for sensory deprivation or isolation. One young man walked by wearing large headphones that for me, evoked a sudden nostalgia for the seventies, eight-track tapes, clicking through the tracks late at night, the innocent post-war/pre-war days—Vietnam/Iraq—of inconsequential sex and drugs, before the twin scourges of Reagan and AIDS. I was a stranger in a strange land.

"We need to talk," my wife said. She was looking at me intently, I knew, even though I was looking not at her but out across the quadrangle admiring the way the bright sun makes the sidewalks shimmer in a brilliant white light. I could feel her looking at me.

"We are talking," I said, continuing to marvel at the shimmer of the sidewalks.

"You know what I mean." Her voice rose in volume and tone. I did know what she meant. She wanted to talk about matters of serious import, of life choices and repercussions, of relationships and children, of time and, of course, though not in so many words, of death.

"I'm tired of talking," I said. And I was. I was so tired I felt as if I could curl up on the beautiful white sidewalk and sleep for a million years, forcing the self-important professors in tweed and designer eyeglasses and the digital undergrads with their digitized lives to step over or around my exhausted body.

"What do you mean by that?" she demanded. "Are you saying you aren't happy?" She fixed me with her most serious scowl, and her voice dropped half an octave, almost into a growl. "Are you seeing someone else? Do you want a divorce?

I sighed again. "It means what it means. I am tired." I thought about how with her there was always a subtext, and without thinking, I said it aloud. "Why always with you there has to be subtext?"

"I live in the subtext," she said. And we sat in a long moment of surprised silence, her words echoing in my mind, and it seemed in hers as well, this unsettling and clearly honest statement. Of course, it was obvious in the harsh light of this afternoon, but I had never before truly realized it, never articulated it, or heard her acknowledge it. We lingered in this bright, little epiphanic moment a while.

Our friends and neighbors and colleagues were all leaving the city it seemed, moving to places that in the past, none of us would have ever before the disaster for a moment considered living. Baton Rouge, Atlanta, Jacksonville. We were among the last of our circle and my wife wanted to join the exodus. She fantasized about places with psychiatrists and functioning stoplights, lingered over Dwell magazine in the checkout line at Whole Foods, ready to trade the once-charming perpetual disrepair of our old Victorian for a modern prefab eco-friendly box. Sometimes then, it was as if she were already there, living her dream life with a baby and a slightly happier, more attentive and kempt version of me, in a glossier zip code someplace else. I had been the one intent on rebuilding. I had been the one who insisted we stay. And so there we were.

I looked at her profile. She was staring off across the quad. She is still attractive, I thought, in the way of women of a certain age, self-assured and stylish, though a little world weary in a way that can also be appealing, perhaps, to someone younger than I, someone less world weary themselves.

"Now we're talking," I said. And for once it seemed, she too was at a loss for words. I stood up, suddenly restless. I swallowed the dregs of my lukewarm coffee. I felt the urge to get behind the wheel of a big goddamn car and drive, but there was only the Civic, which was in the shop again. Wheel bearings and tie rods, the mechanic said. There was a time when I might have tackled the job myself on a Saturday, finding a real manly sense of satisfaction with the chrome Craftsman socket set spread out on the driveway, the car radio playing classic rock, a cold can of cheap beer sweating just within reach. But time passed and somewhere along the line, many other things needed fixing, things not so simply addressed, and these days I seemed to have neither the time nor the inclination.

I had reached the point where I didn't even change my own oil, sitting silently in the Honda at the Five-Minute

Oil Change, sipping complimentary warm root beer in a paper cup and catching up on paperwork while a couple of greasy tattooed kids joked and changed the oil, giving my car the cursory twenty-one-point safety check while speaking a language I once had understood, of cars and girls and illicit drugs the names of which I no longer recognized.

"What are you thinking about?" my wife said.

"Nothing." I tossed the empty Styrofoam cup into a nearby trash receptacle. "I suppose I should get back to work." I envisioned my cubicle.

"I should be going, too." She tilted her head and looked at me with a mixture of curiosity and concern. "Are you okay?"

I shrugged. "A little tired, that's all." The afternoon was waning, and I was thinking happy hour. Another hour or so and I could slip away to a low-ceilinged bar for a draft or two on my way home. Then I remembered I would need a ride home. But for some reason I didn't say anything to my wife, who had the other car. It seemed more effort than I could muster in that moment. She leaned in wearily and I gave her a practiced kiss.

"Can you get dinner on your own? I may be late tonight," she said as she turned to walk away. "A late meeting."

"Sure," I said. The insistent warning beep of a delivery truck backing up sounded somewhere nearby. A groundskeeper wearing large hearing protectors started a gas-powered leaf blower and began to beautify the quadrangle, herding leaves and litter into a little dusty storm of debris.

I watched my wife walking away down the wide concrete walkway and felt a pang I couldn't quite identify. Something bitter yet sweet. A variety of love? A small realization? I was too tired to parse the feeling and it dissipated, leaving a lingering sense of foreboding in its wake. I wondered, is she going to leave me after all? It felt as if an imperceptible crack had appeared in the bright world around me. I walked towards the brick building in which my cubicle waited. I continued walking past it. I walked past the library and the parking garage and out onto the public street where I turned and made my unhurried way toward a small, dark neighborhood bar which I'd passed by many times but into which I had never ventured.

* * *

Dark wood paneling, patinaed brass rail, and a long bar top polished to a high sheen by years of anonymous lives. I nodded to the bartender, a cheerful woman with a lazy eye who pretended that she knew me.

"I've seen you in here before," she said with a smile.

"Perhaps," I said. She smiled and waited, but I had nothing more to say, and she slowly made her way back to the other end of the bar where a couple more gregarious drunks awaited. I watched her in sad admiration.

After a few beers, I realized that what I needed was a walk. I needed to move. I walked out into the late afternoon sun and immediately I was sweating. I loosened my necktie and inhaled deeply. After a few blocks, I removed it completely as I strode briskly down the tree-lined street. Cars periodically clattered past on the potholed street, but in the heat of the day I had the broken, littered sidewalk to myself as if the city were abandoned. I stumbled alone, up and over slabs of concrete heaved up by the roots of ancient trees. At some point, I draped my necktie over a picket fence as I walked by. I could feel my heart pounding in my ears.

I continued walking. I walked until I found myself on the outskirts of the city at dusk in a neighborhood that I did not recognize, and I continued walking still. I realized

I was still carrying my briefcase. It contained important papers regarding the marketing campaign for which I was responsible, a legal pad, a rollerball gel pen, a small voice recorder that I did not like to use, a granola bar and a bottle of water. I stopped in the parking lot of a vacant furniture store. I set the briefcase on an empty newspaper box, opened it and removed the granola bar and the bottle of water. I closed the briefcase and left it there. I walked on, my mind uncluttered with anything but the business of lifting one foot and moving it forward, and then repeating the process likewise with the other. I ate the granola bar. I drank the water. Within an hour or so I was walking through unfamiliar neighborhoods in a city in which I'd spent fifteen years of my life. The sidewalks cracked and heaved beneath my feet in a familiar way, but the houses and street signs were ones I did not recognize. I continued on in what I sensed was a northwesterly direction. I seemed to be walking slightly up hill. The sun began to drop in the sky, the light changed, and I walked on.

I crossed the interstate after scaling a chain-link fence, narrowly dodging a tractor trailer transporting products to a Wal-Mart somewhere. I was feeling a new kind of exhaustion and some exhilaration. I walked along the shoulder of a two-lane blacktop. Occasionally a pickup truck would pass, and sometimes a voice would shout something as it passed. Once a half-empty can of beer hurtled out the passenger window and tumbled harmlessly into the ditch not very near me.

I walked into, through, and out of one small town and then another. Each was different in subtle ways and yet very much the same. The same restaurants, the same grocery stores, the same gas stations. The same dark taverns with slightly different and clever names. The Office Bar, Third Base, The Sportsman's Club, The Crow Bar. The familiar neon beer signs were alluring but I kept on. I had miles to go and so I went.

I slept at night and began walking again with the sun. I recall moments, small details of the surprising debris I passed, the detritus of the American road. Flotsam, I thought, if this were an ocean. Roadkill, the sublime grotesquery of death and decay. A grinning possum not playing dead outside Lafayette, a deer still graceful in its final terror against a concrete interstate retaining wall. And all the lost feral dogs struck by cars and trucks on the highways and byways of Texarkana. I passed a suitcase in the ditch near Omaha. I walked on, carrying with me the mystery of what it might have contained. I was traveling light. I saw the country at the molecular level. It was a different vantage than flying over it. The tidy grid, the lovely quilt at twenty-thousand feet, disappears on foot. I watched ants swarming a half-eaten burger in the gravel while in the distance cattle shuffled in the slurry of a feedlot.

I walked on until I stopped, for no particular reason, in a small city like many other small cities somewhere in the middle. And in that way I found my way out of the predicament that was my life at that time, and into the predicament that is now my life, a predicament so completely different that my previous life seems like a not entirely unpleasant dream from which I recently awoke, the details of which are now fading as I sit here drinking coffee alone at a Formica table littered with beer cans and cigarette butts in a milk glass ashtray, squinting at a crumpled bus schedule and thinking for some reason about a park bench on the quadrangle, warmed by the cruel sunlight that streams in through the smudged kitchen window in this nondescript apartment in a city upriver that still seems strange to me when I wake up in it to find myself here, alone, and no longer really there.

121

Breaking It Down

Every time I turned around it seemed that someone was killing a pig. I met Francine for coffee uptown and she told me about a new restaurant where patrons watch butchers break down pigs as they eat. That's what they call it, she told me, breaking them down. But breaking didn't sound quite right to me. The process must involve a cleaver and sharp knives, breaking an animal carcass down into meat. Perhaps dismantling, I said, though that suggests something that was once assembled, a machine, and not a living creature. As we finished our coffee and scones, I suggested the word butchering might be more accurate, but Francine demurred. The word *butcher* has come to have such negative connotations, she said, a title often conferred on murderers of the serial sort, or those of especially brutal means. The Butchers of Rostov, of Bosnia, of Plainfield, Cadiz, Lyon, New York, Uganda, Kingsbury Run. The Butcher of Mid-City, I added, though of course one would hardly lump a restaurateur in with that lot.

Riptide

Sven Demers stood in the bright afternoon sun at a faded mailbox at the end of a driveway of crushed oyster shells that lead to a tarnished Airstream trailer that had not seen the open road since he'd parked it there upon his arrival in south Florida almost thirty years earlier. He stared at the invitation. His high school reunion, the fortieth. He felt himself unmoored. It seemed a lifetime ago he'd escaped northern Wisconsin and drove south, and perhaps it had been. He rarely thought of Stone Lake but found himself unexpectedly carried along on a wave of odd nostalgia, old memories, and longing.

He realized gradually that he was excited by the prospect of a return to Stone Lake, though it had been years since he'd ventured further north than Gainesville. Wouldn't it be great to show those peckerwoods what Sven Demers had made of himself! He pictured himself pulling into the old school parking lot in his customized Dodge van, longboard prominently displayed on the roof rack. The jocks and cheerleaders, the teachers' pets. He could see them all, now old fools in decline, dragged down by high interest rates, ungrateful offspring, acid reflux, and erectile dysfunction. By God, he would go to this shindig. All he needed was a date, someone youthful and fine draped over his arm. Their toothless jaws would hit the floor. Sven savored the image. He had not been home since his mother's funeral.

Back inside the Airstream he circled the date on the wall calendar, a week after the Lifeguard Certification course, the thought of which dampened his spirits some.

* * *

Sven might never have met Bebel Lundquist but for the expiration of his Red Cross Lifeguarding Certification, which compelled him to take the course once again, as he was required to do every four years, to renew the credentials that allowed him to work for Palm Beach County Park and Recreation as head lifeguard at Boynton Beach. It was a small indignity, Demers felt, this two-week class at the local swimming pool. He, a decorated war vet and legendary lifeguard sitting through videos on life-saving techniques with a sorry group of high school kids, swim-team has-beens, surf punks, and college kids looking to make a few bucks, get a tan, and get laid over the summer. It demeaned his profession, his very being.

The old lifeguard turned heads wherever he went, a physical oddity not easily categorized. Baldheaded, his skull looked like an old warhead, one covered in leather, cracked, discolored, and deeply creased. His small eyes were sunk deep into this hide where they burned like two cigarettes on a moonless night. From the neck down he looked like an ancient health club weight room poster, a strange scarred and weathered youthfulness with each muscle group defined and toned. And there were tattoos: a blue shark circling his left ankle, a Sailor Jerry hula girl on his right bicep, and a rosebud on the left side of his chest.

He cut a striking figure on the white wooden lifeguard tower, a sort of predatory savior, a man of surprising years for his profession. He considered lifeguarding a calling, a profession deserving of the same respect as other such lines of work—emergency medical technician, ER doctor, stunt man, helicopter pilot. In Vietnam, he'd envied the chopper pilots most. He had poor vision in one eye, and had been denied flight school, so young Sven Demers had ridden out the war on a naval supply ship. His combat had been limited to barroom brawls while on leave in Hong Kong, and the occasional loosing of ordnance onto tropical vegetation and small native watercraft along the coast.

*　*　*

Sven arrived on the first day of the Red Cross Lifeguarding Certification class fifteen minutes late, leaving in his wake a palpable aura of tobacco, vodka, and disdain. He took a seat at the top and back of the poolside bleachers while the instructor, a tall, muscled woman in her thirties with close-cropped hair continued the course introduction, ignoring the old lifeguard's late arrival. He scanned the group from behind his mirrored sport shades. He was arrested by the vision of a serious young woman in a bright yellow one-piece. She sat at the end of the bleacher, second row, looking earnest, apparently oblivious to her own beauty. She had a small birthmark on her right thigh, high on the leg and a little to the inside. Sven sat at the back of the class, eyeing the women in the class, calculating relative accessibility, taking note of physical characteristics, distinguishing features.

Bebel, the woman with the birthmark, he learned, was from Brazil, daughter of a Rio socialite and a Swedish importer. She was divorced and did manicures in Boca Raton. She drove a red Isuzu Rodeo. She liked to dance. She'd gone skydiving naked once back in Rio. All of this Sven gathered from Bebel herself in the pool. He'd maneuvered into position as her partner for lifesaving techniques.

They took turns towing each other the length of the pool. A hip nestled into the small of the back, left arm firmly across the chest, and a slow, steady sidestroke to safety.

*   *   *

Sven had been a fearless swimmer as a boy in the lakes and rivers of northern Wisconsin. He'd secretly read Melville and London, dreamt of the sea, and kept to himself. He enlisted in the Navy when he turned eighteen. During his first tour of duty, he acquired a reputation on board. He liked to swim off the ship, naked but for a twelve-inch commando knife strapped to his left thigh. Even the sharks left him alone, he claimed. He re-enlisted for a second tour coaxed by the signing bonus, which he spent on a Pontiac GTO.

When he returned from Vietnam, he got the GTO out of storage. He washed and waxed and buffed it until the lacquer looked like a black hole you could dive into and disappear. He worked the local swimming pool by day and tore up the back roads at night in the GTO, racing all comers for cash and titles.

It was raining the night Sven was driving a young coed home from the casino through the Bad River Reservation at high speed. The big Pontiac started to hydroplane, and he counter-steered instinctively but his reflexes were slow. The car slid sideways, for a ways, down Highway 2, then down into the ditch, carving a wide swath through the vegetation before rolling over three times and coming suddenly to rest upside down against a culvert. Sven crawled from the wreckage unharmed for the most part. His passenger, the daughter of his high school football coach, did not.

Sven felt a deep anguish over the girl's death. He returned home. He began swimming laps every day for hours on end, as if performing some physical penance. He soon spent more time swimming, and less on dry land. He worked overtime and double shifts. He gave up muscle cars and speed, walking to and from the local pool, a shuffling outcast.

One night in the parking lot of the pool, he was jumped by the football coach and a few others. He did not raise a hand to defend himself and took a serious beating. He felt he deserved it and he almost relished the pain. The men kicked him into unconsciousness.

When Sven was able to check himself out of the hospital, he did so. He bought a used Dodge panel van, packed a few clothes and souvenirs, a Navy-issue flare gun, and headed south. He drove for three days, and finally stopped in a sleepy town called Delray Beach. He rented a room inland, but near enough to the Atlantic coast to smell the salt in the cooling breezes that wafted across the hot asphalt and a row of fading palms.

He got a job lifeguarding for the county on the public beaches. He bought a surfboard at a pawnshop and learned to ride it. He fell in love with the bubbly daughter of a golf pro, and they had a baby girl they named Claire. Sven taught his daughter to swim and she was happiest in the water. The family spent long days on the beach, Claire and her daddy frolicking in the waves while Claire's mother sunbathed and read thick paperback novels with colorful embossed covers. The world looked different to Sven after Claire, and he settled into a life that was routine and comfortably pleasant. He worked at being a father, and husband. He came straight home from work. He helped around the house. He put the toilet seat down. He drank a single beer in the evening on the patio with his wife, and watched the sun set on a seemingly endless series of warm days stringing themselves one after the next like so many pearls.

The summer before Claire started school, Sven took her to the beach while his wife went shopping. It was a hazy day, the ocean gray and deceptively calm. Sven was chatting up, in a neighborly way, a couple of girls sunbathing nearby, keeping one eye on little Claire who was playing at the edge of the surf.

He heard a cry for help and saw a woman pointing out at a boy on a bright green inflatable alligator forty yards or so offshore and moving rapidly out to sea. Riptide, Sven thought, as he leapt to his feet and sprinted toward the water. He later recalled that as he ran, he'd savored an acute consciousness of himself, his tan and muscular legs pumping across the sand. He'd sensed the teen-aged girls watching. He ran into the surf, raising his knees high as the water got deeper, his feet exploding into and out of the water. He felt bulletproof. He saw the lifeguard, in his peripheral vision, running into the water down the beach some distance away, an orange flotation device in his hand.

The boy and the alligator continued to drift out. When Sven could not run any further, he dove into the water and began swimming in strong, steady strokes, pulling himself toward the raft. He felt the adrenaline rushing through his body, the metallic taste of fear and excitement. The current was taking the boy, and Sven was not sure he could reach him, but he pushed the doubts from his mind and swam. He swam into each incoming wave, coming up for air infrequently. He felt stronger as he went, faster and more graceful beneath the waves, and soon he could no longer be seen from the beach. The lifeguard had tired and slowed, still kicking out toward the boy receding on the raft, but slowly now, pushing the buoy out in front of him.

Sven surfaced near the boy, circled behind him, and secured him. He swam parallel to the shore until they were released from the riptide, and began to sidestroke in to shore, one arm clamped around the boy and his alligator. Sven's heart was pounding as if it might burst, and he was filled with the euphoria he had always felt in the face of death, a euphoria that conjured up the black waters of Southeast Asia, and the dotted white line disappearing beneath the muscular hood of the GTO as it swallowed miles of Wisconsin backroad blacktop. The thrill of the rescue was tinged with the bittersweet knowledge that no one is ever truly saved for good.

Onshore, a small crowd had gathered to watch the drama, and a spattering of applause erupted when it became clear that the boy had been saved. Sven swam slowly in with the boy on the raft, breathing deeply, returning to the world.

It wasn't until he reached the shore, and he handed the boy over to his distraught mother, that Sven thought of Claire. The stretch of beach where he'd left her was deserted. The teenage girls had wandered over to join the crowd. His beach towel fluttered from the empty chair, and he saw Claire's beach ball bobbing back and forth in the surf at the edge of the shore. Claire was nowhere to be seen.

Sven ran down the beach and back into the water, unaware of anything but a great aching emptiness growing in his chest. He was exhausted but threw himself back into the ocean with a manic fury. He ran up and down the shoreline in the shallow surf, looking frantically in all directions, calling out his daughter's name.

The search and rescue squad arrived. A half hour later, they recovered Claire's body. Two men lifted her small body into the boat and wrapped her in a blanket. When they brought her back to shore, Sven attacked the boat, landing several blows and breaking both of his hands on the gunnel before two paramedics could tackle him, hold him down and sedate him.

His wife filed the divorce papers on the day after Claire's funeral. Sven did little but drink for months, until finally, unable to achieve the relief he sought, he began to swim again. He swam single-mindedly and for great periods of time. He pushed himself, swimming until his skin began to harden and shimmer. He swam underwater for greater and greater distances, finding elusive moments of something like peace there beneath the surface. And he sought to prolong those moments, swimming underwater the length of the pool, and then longer, until he could hold his breath for two lengths, and then more. He swam in the pool and in the ocean. He smelled strongly and always of chlorine and salt.

Gradually, the pain receded though it never went away. Sven began to rebuild his life. He returned to work. He returned to drinking, though in a kind of moderation. And finally, he returned to women, pursuing them with the same vengeance with which he swam.

Years passed. Sven became a fixture, a character, local color. He was the best damn lifeguard on the Atlantic coast. He was a freakish tragic hero who'd survived his own ruin, and no one knew quite what to think about him. Over the years he saved thirteen people from drowning—children, retirees, housewives, and a corpulent Coca Cola executive from Atlanta. He received awards and commendations, his unsmiling picture in the Palm Beach Post, a lifetime supply of Coke, four cases delivered to his door each month by the local distributor. Rumor had it that Sven also slept with an impressive number of women, local and vacationing, youthful and aging, though there was a marked tendency toward the latter, and the former.

* * *

The lifeguarding class became tan as the long sun-drenched days passed and they swam laps in the Olympic-sized pool, treading water for long intervals while holding a diving brick up like an offering. Their body fat percentage dropped and their lung capacity increased. They began to look like lifeguards. Even Sven had to admit to himself that some of the group might be worthy of the profession after all. The week before the test, they met not at the pool, but at a local beach.

The ocean, Sven told Bebel as the class walked to the shore, is a different animal than a swimming pool. Sand, saltwater, breakers, sharks, and riptides. The ocean is a beast, he said. The sun glared off the ragged waves.

Bebel did well in the ocean, the saltwater increasing her buoyancy. But as the class began partner exercises, a storm darkened the sky, miles out but moving in fast. The wind picked up, the yellow flag above the lifeguard tower snapping sharply in the wind. The instructor whistled them in and announced she was ending class.

A red flag replaced the yellow, and in no time the beach was nearly empty. The waves were picking up nicely, approaching four feet at times. Sven retrieved his surfboard from the van. He paddled out into the surf where he put on a little demonstration on riding the waves. Bebel took a turn on the surfboard, tumbling less or more gracefully. The sun was setting, throwing deep reds and yellows off the gathering storm clouds. They climbed a closed-up guard tower and sat legs dangling on the narrow platform to watch. They talked about the usual things, their lifeguard classmates, selected stories from their pasts, trivial details of the present. Bebel turned toward Sven, the evening sun setting her aglow, the wind tossing her fine blonde hair. Sven admired her for a moment, her temporal beauty. She seemed to be presenting herself for kissing.

It was a nice kiss. He figured she was late twenties. She lightly traced her fingertips across the small handprint tattooed over his heart. He considered telling her about it, about the one he hadn't saved, about the little girl who would have been almost her age. But it seemed to him that if he started to tell the story, it wouldn't stop, and he could imagine himself unraveling his entire reckless life, all the wreckage, unveiled for her, and him, to see. He said nothing and they watched the sun easing into the dark Atlantic. He knew she too would soon be gone. He would not take her to Wisconsin to flaunt before his sorry past. He would not do that to her. He imagined himself pulling into the high school parking lot alone, a lonely leathery old fool with an earring and a surf punk's van. He imagined the whispers recounting that night on the Bad River Road, the name of the football coach's daughter in his ears for the first time in all these years. And he decided then he would not be going back for the damn reunion. He would not go back.

Bebel shook a cigarette from the pack and they managed to light it, huddling together in the wind, cupping their hands and their bodies around a cheap red lighter. She exhaled and offered it to Sven. He accepted it, inhaled, and handed it back. Though not a smoker, he sometimes smoked and enjoyed it. He had always liked the smell of tobacco smoke in the air outdoors at night. Bebel seemed calm, content even. They smoked and listened to the steady, soothing pounding of the surf, watched the glow from the sunset burn out into nothing and the horizon disappear into the approaching storm, and Sven felt his restlessness growing.

The waves became louder, and the whitecaps flashed dimly in the distance like cryptic signals of some kind. Sven stood and flicked the cigarette out onto the beach, a shooting star too small for wishing. Sven looked out into the vast darkness and something fell into place within him, something small but significant, an intricate piece of the machinery. He walked back across the sand toward the van, resolute.

Sven returned to the beach with the flare gun. He handed it to Bebel and gave her instructions on its use. He walked out into the surf, pushing the surfboard ahead of him. When he could no longer walk, he lay on the board and paddled steadily out. The water was warm, the air cooling. He checked his dive watch, squinting to see its luminous hands. In ten minutes, Bebel would fire a flare out over the ocean, as he'd directed, and Sven would ride the largest wave he could catch beneath the slow falling umbrella of bright yellow light from the flare, to ride it as far as he could into the inevitable blackness that would follow and swallow him whole. He was going into the belly of the beast, to see if it would spit him out at last, and where.

*　*　*

Sven paddles out on the surfboard, imagining himself riding the big wave, turning the board back into it, entering the wave and being carried away by it. He will lose the surfboard and then he will be swimming, perhaps naked, his trunks torn from his body by the force of the wave, the only sound the roar of the water all around him. He will swim beneath the surface and away from the tiny figure on the beach. After the flare has died, there will be no light, only the faint bleeding of the stars and the distant light pollution from the endless stretch of condos and hotels and strip malls that reach forever north and south along the thin strip of sand at the edge of the continent.

He swims but does not surface. He swims until he becomes swimming, until there is nothing left but his body doing what he has trained it to do, pulling itself through water, taking him further into the great cold embrace of the Atlantic. His entire life has brought him to this moment and he feels a kind of peace. He has no fear. Ahead of him lies another shore. Heaven or hell, he imagines it looks a little like Rio. There may be a lifeguard on the stand there ever vigilant, watching and waiting, but Sven knows all he needs to know of saving, and his heart swells as he swims on.

New Mexico

Two brothers drive a two-lane blacktop west in a pick-up truck and the cab seems to get smaller with each mile marker that flashes past. Their youngest brother is living, last they heard, in New Mexico. They try to think ahead to a state beyond this alien one, conjure up familiar images like the moon rising, a cinderblock motel, a steakhouse, a liquor store. They shift their legs, unable to get comfortable, unable to imagine what lies ahead, the high rolling plains, sagebrush, rock, a lunar landscape with underground concrete bunkers built to store ballistic missiles, the skeletal remains of decommissioned aircraft broken down for salvage or abandoned along a weed-stricken runway, the familiar stranger who sits in a lawn chair smoking a cigarette outside a house he bought on a shuttered air force base, lost in his thoughts, unaware of their approach, gazing north at the lights of Roswell.

The Occasional Palmetto

A commotion in the classroom, several girls shrieking in dismay, retrieved Miss Hester from a momentary flight of fancy. In the midst of the female distress sat Billy Masterson looking unperturbed. The fourth graders had been filling out a worksheet on archeology and early Native American culture in the Florida Panhandle. Miss Hester glared. Billy furrowed his brow in a parody of concentration and filled in the next blank on his worksheet.

Miss Hester told the girls to return to their work and walked back to Billy's desk. She stood beside him with her hand outstretched expectantly.

"What?" said Billy, all wide-eyed innocence. "I ain't got nothing."

"Don't have anything," said Miss Hester. "And don't lie to me. Let's have it."

There were muffled snickers elsewhere in the classroom, but Miss Hester kept her gaze on Billy. She had no idea what the boy had this time. She knew he was behind the disruption and would bet her teaching certification that some contraband was involved. Billy tried to meet her look, but his earnest mask of innocence cracked. He was getting better, though, she noted. By the time the hormones kicked in, he'd be able to lie straight faced with some success. She imagined him in a high school letter jacket, still disrupting the girls, charming them into the back of his parent's minivan and out of their day-of-the-week panties. She knew his kind.

Miss Hester returned to her desk, inspecting the fake vomit, marveling at its rubbery verisimilitude. It was amazing what they could do with injection molding these days. She dropped the novelty into the bottom right-hand desk drawer with the impressive collection of action figures, water pistols, and pocketknives she had amassed. She liked to tell the students that the confiscated items went to her boyfriend, who loved such things. Upon appropriating a particularly nice slingshot, or a Day-Glo Uzi, Miss Hester would exclaim: "Oh, this is nice! Rhett has been wanting one of these!"

The students speculated amongst themselves on the playground. Miss Hester was the oddest teacher in the school. She was older than some of their parents it was rumored, and not married nor even divorced. Though she still looked hot, Billy would add, for an old maid. Of course Rhett existed only in Miss Hester's imagination, a fictional suitor she'd created as an answer to the awkward questions of students, other teachers, and people in the community. In Panacea, a single woman her age was a rarity. And she did not attend church, verifying the locals' perceptions of people from the city. She was so nice, folks would say, and a good teacher, but you know, she did go to school in New Orleans. She didn't seem interested in any of the local bachelors, of which there were a few. And of course, she'd grown up in the North. Rhett had begun as something of a joke, a silly fantasy with which to divert the small-town nosiness. But as their relationship entered its third year, Miss Hester found it less amusing, as sometimes happens with relationships.

* * *

The last bell rang, and Wendy nearly skipped to her car, the bright red shine of it stirring her heart to quicken. She started the engine and relished its rumbling idle. She slid a compact disc by the Heartbreakers into the dash, undid her ponytail, and shook loose a head full of curly red hair. She accelerated out of the parking lot onto the road with a little more enthusiasm than she intended, and the rear wheels of the Camaro chirped as they launched her forward. She was going to the beach at Pensacola for the weekend.

After all, she sang along, *it's a great big world with places to run to*. The sun beat down with summertime intensity, though it was already the end of September. Wendy tilted the rearview mirror and applied lipstick. She appraised herself briefly and frowned at the small lines that had appeared at the corners of her eyes. She put on her sunglasses, turned up the music, and headed for the interstate. She'd packed her bags the night before.

*   *   *

Wendy checked into a Drury Inn with an overnight bag containing a bottle of vodka and a bottle of Bloody Mary mix she'd bought when she crossed the county line, and a paperback novel. She couldn't bring herself to buy liquor in Dothan and have alcohol added to the townspeople's list of her perceived flaws. She changed into a stylish yet modest one-piece and headed for the beach. The sun was dropping toward the offshore oil rigs to the west, and a few sun-burned tourists dragged themselves and their gear through the sand to their cars. By the time Wendy got to the beach, it was nearly deserted. She applied sunscreen, lit a Marlboro Light 100, and opened a trim novel called *The Moviegoer*. As the nicotine rushed to her head, she leaned back on the beach towel to read.

No one at the school knew that she smoked cigarettes and she wouldn't smoke them in the Camaro. She was still savoring the new car smell two years later. Her first new car. All things considered it had gotten to be a challenge for her to smoke her half pack a day these days. She wanted to quit, but on her own terms. She worried about gaining weight if she quit. She walked a mile every day after school, the round-trip distance to the video store, and she was not in bad shape she figured. Though she wondered why she bothered in Panacea. The only available men were unemployed, recently paroled, or still living with their mothers. The book fell closed and Wendy closed her eyes to daydream about Rhett.

Of course, Wendy's Rhett was not the quintessential southern gentleman his name might imply, but a complex man of beguiling contradictions: rough yet sensitive, an intellectual but down-to-earth, a kind of modest renaissance man who'd appreciate the irony of a name like Rhett. In a word, exactly not the man with whom she'd lived for three years in Tampa, where she'd landed her first teaching job. That was a real estate developer with a taste for Hollywood blockbusters, cocaine and teenage prostitutes.

Wendy had come home from school sick one day to their bay front condo and found him on their white leather sofa with a skinny girl whose dark roots were showing through the blonde. The girl was wearing Wendy's bathrobe, a nice bathrobe she'd gotten at a nice hotel in West Palm Beach. There was a small pile of white powder on the glass coffee table, a bottle of champagne and two of their good flutes.

The job in Panacea had seemed the answer, a cure-all, and for the first two years it had been. She'd thrown herself into her teaching and she enjoyed living in her very own house however modest. She missed the beach but drove to Pensacola for a weekend every few months to get away, swim and sunbathe. For a time, this had been enough. But she'd become restless and this fantasy man she'd created for the benefit of her students had become a presence away from school, apparently no longer satisfied with confiscated toys from her desk drawer. He seemed to want more from her, and she more from him.

*　*　*

When Wendy awoke, the sun was gone and the western sky was ablaze. The air had cooled and she had chill bumps on her arms and legs. The beach was empty but for a lone figure who appeared to be jogging towards her on the wet sand at the water's edge. By the time she gathered up her towel and beach bag, the runner was going past. A man in his late forties, she guessed, close-cropped graying hair, but fit for his age. She deliberately looked away and ran her hands through her hair. The jogger slowed. She faltered, and became conscious of the cut of her swimsuit, the exposed flesh of her thighs. Wendy quick stepped into a pair of faded Tulane gym shorts and pulled on a T-shirt. When she glanced toward the surf again, the man was gone down the beach, his footprints fading in the wet sand. She was relieved some, and her heart sank some.

The next day Wendy checked out of the motel and drove east in a state of vague nostalgia. The beach suddenly seemed endless, the Gulf too immense to endure alone. She stopped in Apalachicola and walked through an overgrown antebellum cemetery complete with Confederate War memorial. She stopped into a tourist art gallery and was overcome with existential despair and a powerful thirst.

Evening approached and she drove on. She passed a roadhouse called The Sand Bar, half hidden beside a two-lane bridge over the Wakulla River. She slowed and glanced at the improbable two-story structure with a Dixie Beer sign in the window and drove on. Stopping finally at Knight's Rest, a 1950s vintage motor court with a faux medieval theme. The place seemed to be run by a family of East Indians, the lobby infused with curry. Or perhaps they were Pakistani. Wendy could not recall the details of the social studies unit on the peoples of the Middle East. The curry smelled great, and she wished they'd invite her to join them for dinner in the mysterious back room curtained off behind the front desk. A prominently displayed sign said that spelled out in elegant script, United We Stand, over an American flag. From the back room a television murmured. It sounded like the Weather Channel.

Wendy dropped her bags in the room. She was restless and thirsty. She went outside and got back into the Camaro and drove west. She passed several of the bars on the state highway, but they looked false and cheerful and if she had not slowed to gape at a dead pig lying on the shoulder at the edge of the bridge, all four feet pointing skyward, she well might not have driven past The Sand Bar again.

Wendy liked the place immediately for its lack of flair, for its rust-streaked tin sign weathered almost indecipherable, for the great weeping willow that leaned over the unpainted building and obscured the tavern's dim neon from the bridge that crossed the small muddy river which the parking lot overlooked.

She parked the Camaro on the far side of the lot under the mercury vapor light. She counted five pickups and two minivans. She checked her look in the mirror on the sun visor and took a deep breath. Her hips swayed as she walked to the entrance in a way that they did not when she was walking to the video store in Crawfordville. She was unusually aware of the tight fit of her jeans, the feel of fabric on her skin after the day in the sun on the beach. She felt just a little bit dangerous.

She chose a barstool in the corner. Merle Haggard was singing Big City on the jukebox. A woman was working behind the bar in a black T-shirt with a bandanna gathering most of her dark hair. She was of indeterminate age and race was shucking the fresh oysters with a short, blunt-tipped knife and sliding them onto a battered metal tray. The oysters were spilling onto a stainless-steel back bar from a fifty-pound burlap sack, wet, rough, and good-sized. The woman wore a cotton work glove on her non-dominant hand and Wendy watched her for a while. She was good with the oyster knife.

Wendy ordered a beer, and the woman brought her a bottle of Corona. She nodded at the sack of oysters. "The best oysters around, honey," she said. "Fresh from Apalachicola."

"Sure," Wendy said, "Why not?"

The barmaid placed in front of Wendy then the tray of oysters. She slid a bottle of Tabasco and a red plastic basket of saltines next to the tray. "Enjoy."

"Thank you," said Wendy as she prepared the first oyster.

* * *

A tug on her sleeve caused Wendy to tense, an oyster half swallowed. She heard a small voice say, "Hey." She finished swallowing and chased the oyster with a quick gulp of beer before turning on her bar stool. There seemed to be nobody there. Then she saw the top of a small head with frizzy dark hair.

"Quarters for the jukebox, ma'am?" The girl made eye contact and held out a small hand. "I like Patsy Cline, do you?"

"I do," Wendy admitted. She had imagined walking after midnight with Rhett, arm in arm in the moonlight. She fumbled into her purse for some change. "What's your name?"

"Tallulah," the child replied, "but everyone calls me Lula for short. Except my daddy who calls me Little Lady."

Wendy watched Lula skip to the jukebox, feed in the coins, and solemnly press the buttons. The machine whirred, and sure enough, Patsy Cline began to sing. Lula waltzed back to Wendy smiling and held out her hand. In the girl's small palm lay an arrowhead.

"This is for you," said Lula.

Wendy took the arrowhead and turned it over in her hand, admired the craftsmanship and thought about the hundreds of years, the lost culture it represented. It was in remarkable condition, its edges still sharp. "Thank you," she said.

Lula waltzed away across the room and climbed onto a bar stool beside an unshaven man in a faded camouflage fatigue jacket. Wendy watched them in the mirror behind the bar. Her mind wandered. Rhett, back from the war, quietly refused to talk about the horror, and for Wendy, the deep, blue pain of it became the color of his eyes. She both feared and desired the beautiful mysteries behind those eyes. She longed to heal his wounds. She was a bit tipsy she realized. Bumper stickers and placards festooned the tavern walls. A black flag commemorated soldiers missing in action. A Confederate battle flag emblazoned with a Gothic forget, hell.

The barmaid followed Wendy's gaze. "Lots of vets come in here." She pulled off the glove and lay it beside the oyster knife. She lit a cigarette and flexed her hands. "Some work at the marina. Some are pot hunters." She nodded at the arrowhead that lay the bar.

"Pot hunters?"

The barmaid looked around the room and lowered her voice. "Indian stuff. Pots, arrowheads, what have you. There's old Indian burial mounds all over this part of the panhandle."

"Is that legal?"

"Not exactly…" The barmaid turned and began cleaning the oyster knife on an old gray towel. Wendy looked around to see the man in fatigues standing behind her, Lula at his side, clutching his hand.

"This is her, Daddy. She likes Patsy Cline, too."

"Ma'am." The man shuffled his feet in an awkward, endearing sort of way. The jukebox clicked and whirred. Another country western song began with the lonesome twang of a steel guitar. For a moment, Wendy thought he was going to ask her to dance, and her stomach fluttered. Or perhaps it's just the oysters, she thought.

"Get this gal a beer, Thelma." The man called out to the barmaid without taking his eyes off Wendy. "Put it on my tab."

* * *

In retrospect, the events of the rest of the evening were hazy for Wendy. At some point she'd joined the man, Trip, at a rough-hewn table in the back. Their initial awkwardness fell away gradually, thanks to great sweaty pitchers of cheap beer that kept appearing on the table, and to Lula's precocious forthrightness. To a soundtrack of classic southern rock and outlaw country, the evening unfolded pleasantly, and it seemed only natural for Wendy to find herself dancing slowly to the jukebox in the tattooed arms of a man she'd only just met. There was an awkward moment between songs, back at the table. Wendy asked Lula what grade she was in. Fourth, Lula told her. Wendy said that she was a fourth-grade teacher and Lula looked at her in disbelief.

"You are not." Lula said matter-of-factly.

Wendy told Lula about her class. She told her about Billy Masterson and his fake vomit. She told her about her drawer of confiscated toys. But she did not mention Rhett.

The subject of the ancient native culture of the region arose, as it often would. Wendy was surprised to learn he'd been majoring in archaeology before dropping out to enlist. She told him about a field trip to a dig her junior year at Tulane, an excavation at the site of a brothel in Storyville.

Then Trip told Wendy about his nighttime excursions onto federal land in search of burial mounds, his voice hushed. He'd never been caught, he told her, because he had a reverence for these things. He was part Creek himself. He told her how he excavated a site, taking up to a week sometimes, removing each pot with care. Not like others who'd tear into the mounds with nothing more than a pickax and a shovel, destroying much of the pottery just to gather up whatever arrowheads they could easily find, leaving the site exposed. Trip tried to leave the mounds looking as he'd found them.

Wendy was taken aback. This was grave robbing, in a sense. And probably a violation of state and federal statutes.

"It's a living," Trip said.

Later, the subject of pancakes came up. There was talk of a pancake breakfast in the morning. Lula's idea. Trip drew a crude map on the back of a Sand Bar menu. Ten o'clock, they decided. Lula's mother was picking her up at noon to take her home to Tallahassee when her weekend with her daddy was over.

"Promise?" said Lula.

"I promise," Wendy said. What the hell, she thought.

It was late when Wendy walked with Trip, who was carrying his sleeping daughter, to his pick-up truck. He had an odd limp, Wendy noticed. He'd been awkward on the dance floor, but so were most straight men she'd known. She watched him carry Lula slowly across the parking lot, struggling to keep his balance, as if he were still learning how to walk. It did not seem like a drunken walk despite the pitchers of beer.

Trip buckled Lula into a car seat in the front of the pick-up, kissed her, and called her Little Lady. Then he walked with Wendy to her car at the other end of the crushed oyster shell parking lot. They leaned against the Camaro side by side and smoked the day's last cigarette looking up at the moon which appeared to be hung up in a willow tree.

Trip flicked his cigarette away. He mumbled something endearing, turned and fell into Wendy as if making a clumsy attempt to embrace her. He would have fallen had she not caught him. Trip might have blushed. Wendy laughed, and after a moment, he laughed too. He nodded toward his truck where Lulu waited sleeping. "Well," he said, "I guess I better go."

*　*　*

The next morning, Wendy nursed herself back to life beside the motel pool with a Bloody Mary. She unfolded the Sand Bar menu and studied the simply-drawn map. In the bright light of day, it seemed crazy that she'd even talked to the guy, but she felt a little stir again as she recalled details of the previous night. She went for a swim, returned to her room, and showered.

She left the motel and drove to a gas station. A man refueling at another pump caught her eye, vaguely familiar, good-looking in a military recruitment ad sort of way. He caught her looking, and smiled slightly, gave a little nod, not of recognition but of vague civility.

The man jogging on the beach. She smiled and looked at the gas pump. She hoped he'd say something as she passed by on her way into the store. He didn't. Inside, she waited in a line to pay for the gasoline. She glanced at a display of cheap compact discs, skimming the titles. There among the Merle Haggard and All Time Greatest Trucking Songs she saw Patsy Cline.

* * *

She drove inland, just driving she told herself, in the general direction of the oyster bar and coincidentally the small "X" beyond it that represented Trip's home on the crumpled menu that lay on the passenger seat of the Camaro. She drove along a two-lane blacktop county highway lined with anemic pines, roadkill, and the occasional palmetto. She tallied the roadkill, mostly dogs and raccoons, but also armadillos and a large animal that looked like another pig. She wondered if it had fallen off a truck. Or jumped. Pigs were said to be intelligent animals and a pig in the back of a pick-up truck had to know that the trip would not end well.

* * *

If she had not seen the man from the beach again, the well-groomed Rhett Butler of her first evening's brief fantasy on the beach, things might have played out quite differently for Wendy, for Rhett, for Trip, and for Lula. But Wendy did see him, for a third time, standing alongside the road, in the hazy distance beyond the dead pig, the size of a toy soldier, but growing larger as the Camaro approached until there he was. A normal-sized man. Maybe even a little larger than life, standing as if pondering great meaningful questions beside a blue Ford Crown Victoria, smoke trailing from beneath its open hood. Wendy passed by, catching all of this in a flash. She glanced in the rearview for a reverse angle of the situation and slowed to a halt in the gravel on the roadside fifty yards or so beyond the wounded Ford. She looked at her watch. She was due at Trip's in thirty minutes. She looked again in the mirror. Rhett stood waiting on the shoulder of the road behind her.

The Camaro idled with a throaty growl that always gave her a small secret thrill, a deep vibration that pulsed into the leather shift knob she cupped in her hand. She slid the shifter into first gear, turned sharply and accelerated, spinning the car around and back in the direction from which it had come. There was a short squeal from the wide tires as they spun and found traction on the asphalt. She was beside Rhett Butler and the smoking Ford in a flash.

The smoke from under the hood turned out to be steam, and in the sweet fragrance of overheated coolant, Wendy introduced herself to Rhett, whose name it turned out was Neal. He seemed less confident than at the beach, his khakis showing wrinkles and a smear of grease. Neal informed her that he'd called Triple-A but that the wait might be a long one.

"There's a big wreck on the I-10 they said."

"Looks like your fan belt, and radiator hose," called Wendy from under the hood. "You live around here?"

"I'm from Atlanta."

"Vacationing?" Wendy straightened up and walked back to Neal, blowing an errant lock of hair from her face.

"You could say that," he said unconvincingly.

He asked her about herself, following her to the Camaro. Wendy popped the trunk and began her story, the abbreviated first date version replete with self-deprecatory humor and a touch of pathos. Her mother died young, cancer. Her father had been a mechanic. Still was, she corrected herself. He had his own business, such as it was, in Cleveland. She did not mention that he was a recovering alcoholic, an ex-biker, a lapsed Catholic, whom she rarely saw. He'd quit drinking in his thirties, settled into a mean-spirited sobriety, self-righteous and cruel. She'd left for New Orleans on a volleyball scholarship to Tulane, and never looked back.

From the trunk she removed a plastic jug of antifreeze and a ratchet, some sockets, a small pry bar, a roll of duct tape. She then dug into her overnight bag, through the clothes she'd worn to school. She pulled out a pair of nylon stockings.

"This ought to do the trick," she said a little shyly.

A look of slight alarm crossed Neal's face, but he recovered quickly. "I have to be in Panacea. Could you give me a lift? I'll pay you."

Wendy hesitated. She knew enough not to get into a car with a strange man, as a rule. But she also knew that rules were made to be broken. And she was tempted to break this one, and might well have, had he not brought money into the equation. What the hell did she look like, a cab driver? And what could be so important in Panacea? But he wasn't hard to look at, and her fantasy from the beach still clung to him.

She told him that she too had someplace to be and suggested they sit in her car while they waited for his engine to cool. They sat in the Camaro, idling, listening to an oldies station, and it became again like a first date. They talked about current events and told funny stories from high school.

Wendy stopped toying with the mace dangling from her key chain. Neal loosened his navy-blue necktie.

"What do you do for a living?" Wendy asked, having given him a detailed account of her fourth-grade class, which was losing its luster in the re-telling.

"I shouldn't tell you this." He leaned over and lowered his voice. "I'm a federal agent." He said it like it was a pick-up line and judging from his expression, a sly grin, one with which he'd had some success.

Wendy said nothing. Though her relationship with her father was strained, she had inherited, among other things, a healthy distrust of cops, diluted from her father's hatred of them which stemmed, Wendy suspected, from the four-year stretch he did during her late teens for possession with intent to distribute.

"I'm not actually on vacation." Neal said. "I'm here on a job."

Wendy got the impression that he expected her to ask about his job, which he wasn't supposed to talk about but would, in confidence of course, to further implicate her in a growing intimacy. But she remained silent, gazing out the windshield at the heat waves shimmering on the pavement of the empty two-lane highway.

"I'm interested in Indian artifacts," Neal finally admitted.

"Who isn't," said Wendy brightly. "But the proper term is Native American."

"Artifacts dug up on federal land, specifically." Neal smiled. "You wouldn't know where I might find any such artifacts, Native American that is, locally?"

"I surely don't." Wendy got out of the car. What if Neal had been following her? She was suddenly worried for Trip, which surprised her. She'd pondered turning him in herself.

She could take off right now, but that might make him suspicious. Perhaps if she fixed his car, enough to get to the nearest town. "I don't much care for artifacts. I like the uncluttered look. Knickknacks make me crazy. Minimalist, my place. The furniture's all IKEA."

"What?"

"Scandinavian. Simple, clean lines. Modern. Very European." She turned off the radio and removed the keys from the ignition. "I think that radiator has likely cooled."

It took her about twenty minutes to tape the radiator hose, loosen the alternator, fashion a temporary fan belt from her control-top extra-support hose (color: sand), retighten the pulley, and refill the radiator from a gallon jug of water she kept in the trunk of the Camaro, a habit from years of driving high-mileage used cars with salvage titles she bought from her old man. She put away her tools and they stood awkwardly beside the Crown Victoria, which was no longer smoking.

They shook hands, almost formally. Neal gave Wendy an official-looking business card embossed with an eagle clutching a mess of arrows. She gave him a fictitious last name and warned him to keep it under thirty-five miles per hour and have a new fan belt put on first chance he got.

She looked at the clock and thought about Lula. She left the scene in a hurry. She drove fast, and realized she was crying, crying as if she'd just broken it off with a man she had loved for a long time, but with whom it no longer was working. The spark that had brought them together was gone. She felt the heady mix of freedom and grief that comes with the end of a relationship. She wondered if Trip and Lula had waited for her.

* * *

Wendy arrived an hour late at Trip's trailer deep in the woods and parked beneath a huge live oak draped in Spanish moss. A mongrel dog began barking from where it was chained to a wrecked motorcycle with a crumpled front fork and wheel. Trip appeared from an old wooden shed that was unencumbered by paint and had settled into the soft earth unevenly and now leaned against a group of small trash trees that had grown up beside it. He was carrying a large olive drab GI duffel.

"You're late." Trip walked over to his truck and laid the duffel across the passenger side of the bench seat.

"I stopped to help this guy…" Wendy began. "Car trouble, overheated. I'm sorry."

Trip lit a cigarette and dragged on it hard. He looked at Wendy as if seeing her for the first time.

"Lula…" Wendy looked at the house then back at Trip.

"Lula's gone. Her momma come early and got her." He stood beside his truck, jaw clenched. "She was counting on pancakes."

"Wait…" Wendy said. She walked towards the truck.

"You don't break a fucking promise to a kid. You should know that." Trip got in the cab and slammed the door. He looked at her, his arm hanging out the window. "I got business in town."

Wendy felt lightheaded. The day was already hot, insects in the trees buzzing incessantly, the mindless barking of the dog. She realized how much she'd been looking forward to pancakes with the little girl. The dog barked again.

"You know…" she said.

"Shut up," said Trip, to the dog, who barked once more and lay down with its head on its front paws, watching them mournfully.

"I was looking forward to it too."

"Then you should've been here when you said."

"You're right," said Wendy. "I wanted to see you, too."

Trip squinted at her, and she saw creases around his eyes, the wild tangle of hair coming out from under his filthy NASCAR cap. He was no Rhett Butler, but even so she could imagine him cussing her in an exasperated loving sort of way and then sweeping her off her feet.

He started the truck and revved the motor. A cloud of white smoke streamed out the tailpipe.

"You're burning oil," Wendy said, "bad piston rings most likely."

The next thing that happened surprised them both. Wendy walked around to the passenger side and opened the door. She climbed into the truck. She slid across the seat and put an arm around Trip, nestling her face into his neck. He smelled like tobacco and fossil fuel. There was a kiss though it's hard to say who initiated it, a deeply serious kiss. Wendy turned off the ignition and tossed the keys under the seat.

In the course of their passions, Wendy became aware of Trip's right leg against her left. It was unusually solid. She heard him inhale slightly when she put her hand on his thigh and slowly moved down the leg. Just above the knee she stopped, having felt a gap there. It was one of those moments when time slows way down and everything becomes clear, and Wendy knew she'd remember this always, every small detail of it.

"I think you're sweet," said Wendy.

"Sweet?" said Trip.

"Your leg," she said, reverently.

Trip did not reply.

Wendy for some reason recalled a story she'd read in college and stifled a laugh.

"What's so funny?"

"Nothing," said Wendy. "Can we move this little party inside?"

"I do have business in town…" Trip said.

Wendy kissed him hard. "I think it's best you stay here with me."

Trip bit his lower lip and placed his hand on the duffel bag on the seat beside them.

"I'm not a Bible salesman," Wendy said reassuringly.

*   *   *

An hour and a half later, they lay side by side beneath an old air conditioner that rattled above Trip's mattress. From the racket, you'd expect some cool air, but the small room was stifling. Wendy took a small hit off the joint that he had deftly rolled in the afterglow. She coughed and her eyes teared up.

Trip's prosthetic leg, still wearing a muddy jungle boot, leaned rakishly against a wooden chair that was piled high with National Geographic magazines, and a Penthouse or three. Wendy's black brassiere, her best, Victoria's Secret, draped seductively over the top of the leg. It had been a surprise of course, the leg, but she'd recovered nicely. She was neither, she had assured him, narrow-minded nor squeamish. And as things progressed, she found it a new thrill, an addition by subtraction, an erotic first, the first in some time. Trip watched Wendy reclining there in one of his Airborne T-shirts with what you'd have to call admiration.

"I want to see you again. And Lula, too."

"That's up to her." He exhaled a cloud of smoke. "But all right by me."

Wendy took Neal's business card out of her pocket and wrote her real name and number on the back. She handed it face up to Trip.

"You'll want to watch out for this guy." She described Neal and his Crown Vic. "He's got a keen interest in local Native artifacts."

* * *

Wendy left Trip with a note of apology for Lula, and a new compact disc of Patsy Cline's Greatest Hits. She drove home with a warm schoolgirl glow which might have been from a touch of sunburn from her day at the beach. On the passenger seat of the Camaro sat a small pottery dish, circa 200 BC, in unusually fine condition. A missing shard had left an elegant little triangle in the bowl, negative space, a flaw that only made the bowl more attractive to Wendy. She pictured it in her bedroom, a nice counterpoint to the modern decor. Trip had fished the priceless and illegal artifact out of his duffel, the best one, he'd said. She thought about how she might box up the bright collection of toys and other contraband in her school desk drawer and take them to Trip when she returned the following weekend. He'll like that, she thought. She turned up the radio and sang along with "I Fall to Pieces," as she traveled through the flat panhandle landscape lit by the harsh sun to an uncluttered glow.

Carl, Under His Car

Carl, under his car on a Saturday morning, stares at the bell housing of the automatic transmission that has settled heavily onto the left side of his chest, and he thinks about the conversation he had with his wife earlier this morning. The argument was not unusual. This time Angel, their sixteen-year-old daughter, wants to go on a school trip to Washington, D.C. Carl is sure this is not a good idea—a bunch of hormone-crazed teenagers on a three-day trip to a big city with only a handful of chaperones. Three days also means two nights the kids will spend in a hotel. It isn't just the money, though that is no small consideration. The thought of his Angel in a hotel room causes Carl to squirm, and when he does, a sharp pain shoots through his left side. Jesus Christ, he winces. Somewhere deep within him there is a twinge of guilt tinged almost imperceptibly with pleasure. Or vice versa. Sometimes it's as if he'd never left Holy Cross High School.

Gloria left this morning in a huff to spend the day shopping at the local mall. Carl retired to the garage to work on his project—a 1972 Buick Gran Sport in an early stage of restoration. A repair manual lies open on the workbench, grease-smeared fingerprints mark the page for automatic transmission removal and installation. Step 14. Remove the bolts that attach the transmission bell housing to the engine. Step 15. While using a pry bar to ensure that the torque converter stays firmly mounted to the transmission, pull the transmission off the engine.

Carl doesn't recall what the next step is. He does remember that the manual states that installation is basically the reverse of removal. And he is sure the manual does not have specific instructions for removing a transmission that is wedged between the engine and a hapless shade tree mechanic, effectively pinning him under the car. He hears his dead father's voice, the sneer in it when he says the words shade tree mechanic. Carl's father, the auto mechanic. Carl Sr., a real auto mechanic with a closet full of blue work shirts, long and short sleeve, with the "Mr. Goodwrench" patch over the left pocket and his name, Carl, in script above the right.

The garage door gapes open to a mild, sunny day, and Carl worries that one of his neighbors might happen by, see him under the car, and stop to chat. He does not want to chat with any of his neighbors right now, and as much as he would like to be out from under his car, he doesn't much like the idea of asking, say, Bruce Edelbrock for help. He knows he would never hear the end of it. He imagines Bruce down at the Town Tap. *There he was, I tell ya, pinned to the floor under his own car like a goddamn bug. I don't know what woulda happened to him if I hadn't stopped by. Huh. Huh. Huh.* That laugh.

The pain is not too bad, Carl thinks. From where he is pressed to the oil-stained concrete floor, he can see the corner of his workbench, the open toolbox, a wooden shelf bowing under the weight of a row of old baby food jars filled with nails, cotter pins, assorted nuts and bolts. He sees the calendar hanging on the pegboard among the hand tools and extension cords. Even though it is late March, Miss February still smiles warmly in an orange bikini. She stands in glossy living color next to a new Ridgid pipe threader, one hand on her bare hip, the other caressing the sleek machine. Carl looked ahead, into the future, and found Miss March, sultry with a twenty-four-inch pipe wrench, somehow less aesthetically pleasing, and so has been content to remain in February in his garage.

Carl has worked a pipe threader like Miss February's. His brother-in-law, a heating and plumbing contractor, has a similar threader, though his is filthy with cutting oil. It resembles the one on the calendar, well, about like Gloria resembles Miss February, Carl thinks, and immediately he feels a twinge of guilt that is not at all like the pain in his shoulder, nor tinged with pleasure of any kind. Carl loves his wife. He has worked with her brother since being laid off from the canning company, where he'd worked since high school, as he'd always expected to. He lugs the machine from and to the truck during the week and has come to resent the heavy threader.

The underside of the Buick smells of used motor oil and automatic transmission fluid. Smells that remind Carl of his father. Carl, when underneath cars, has never quite shaken the feeling that his father is watching critically his every move. This causes him to try too hard with ratchets and pry bars, to lose his cool when a bolt won't loosen or a wrench slips. Gloria teases that he can't seem to change the oil on one of their cars without barking the skin off his knuckles. And she's more right than Carl would like to admit. All the way back to auto shop. But he finds peace in the garage, under his car. More and more, it has become the only place in his house where he feels at ease. With Angel older, in high school now, Carl has become an outsider in a house of women. He never has understood women, he admits to himself, and they become more and more mysterious to him as time goes on. Carl's mother died when he was a child, of a weak heart, his father had told him.

Carl feels fluid trickle slowly from his shoulder to the inside of his arm and into his armpit. It tickles some, and he hopes it's transmission fluid, a bright viscous red that doesn't look at all like blood. He's afraid to move his arm. He grimaces at the tickle, and imagines how he must look, under his car, grimacing while transmission fluid runs into his armpit, and he laughs, triggering a sharp pain in his chest, like the one he felt when he first tried to move after the transmission slipped off the floor jack onto him. The transmission didn't really fall on him. He'd been almost snug beneath it, trying to free the torque converter with a pry bar when the jack kicked out, and the transmission, a Turboglide, settled into him like a bowling ball into a cheap mattress. Not to imply that Carl is anything like a cheap mattress, though Carl Sr. used to bowl league every Wednesday night at the Stardust Lanes.

Carl closes his eyes to think. The concrete is cold beneath him, and he can hear small sounds. A whir that he identifies as the electric clock on the garage wall. He stole the clock from the plant when he was laid off after twelve years of faithful service. That was what, ten years ago now? How has it come to this? he wonders, the years flying by like mere passing thoughts, like faraway dreams.

In the distance he hears a voice, constant and vaguely familiar. It's Harry Carey, he realizes. Someone in the neighborhood is listening to the Cubs game. They're playing the Reds today. Preseason. Carl thinks the pitching staff is looking better this year, but he isn't too hopeful. Being a Cubs fan, he knows, means maintaining a stubborn glimmer of hope in the face of almost certain disappointment. He tries to make out the radio broadcast, but Harry's words seem to be carried along on the breeze, and only the sound of them is blown into the garage. It would be nice to be able to hear the game while he lays here, he thinks. Carl is not given to panic, and he has not yet begun to worry. Not too much. He is short of breath, but Gloria will be home eventually. He can't see the clock, or the wristwatch on his immobilized left arm, but he figures it is close to noon. Which reminds him that he hasn't eaten since a coffee and Danish this morning. His stomach rumbles.

Carl tries to figure where Gloria might be, to determine when she might be coming home. He pictures her leaving the house this morning. It must have been around ten. She would drive down Palisade to the thrift store, maybe pick up some work clothes for him, an alarm clock for her collection. Half an hour or forty-five minutes there. Then on to the mall. Carl loses her at the mall. He goes there once a year, at Christmas, and it gives him heartburn just to think about it.

Hell, he has no idea where she is, or how long she'll be. She might be out with Jennie Hurst for all he knows. Maybe she and Jennie are at the Continental Lounge across from the mall right now, drinking White Russians and talking about their husbands. Carl doesn't want to think about that possibility. At the last neighborhood cocktail party, Jennie came up to Carl where he stood by the hors d'oeuvres, and ran her long, manicured fingers lightly down his arm and smiled.

"When is that hot rod of yours going to be ready for a test ride, Carl?"

All the while, Henry, her husband, stood across the room watching, leering at them. And Hurst, the school psychologist, was one of the chaperones for the D.C. trip. Which gets Carl back to thinking about Angel. His Angel. Carl remembers like yesterday the day she was born, a little pink bundle in his wife's arms and him feeling like he'd just come awake for the first time in his life, that everything up to this moment suddenly meant nothing. Everything beyond this moment an unwritten book. The universe shifted, and he was no longer at the center of it. This soft little bundle was. When he held her, he realized this was the most important thing he'd ever done, and he swore that he would always be there for her. Always.

But now his Angel is like a stranger to him, listening to that goddamn hip hop music. She rolls her eyes at him when he remarks on the music and the baggy pants, her bare midriff and the blue anodized ring in her pierced navel. She spends hours on the phone and can't utter a sentence without using the word "like" at least half a dozen times. He knows he sounds like his old man, but he can't help himself.

When some kid appears at the door to pick Angel up for a date, Carl makes a point of trying to scare the hell out of him. A dark look, a crushing handshake, his shirtsleeves rolled up over his tattooed, muscled biceps. He knows what is on these boys' minds and he doesn't like it one bit. He remembers getting the same treatment from Gloria's old man when he was their age and it pains him to remember how ineffectual it was, how he had his hands up under her sweater before they were two blocks away.

Carl had another Gran Sport back then. The love of his life. Red with white stripes. All the factory options. The big block 455. Early one February morning coming back from Wisconsin, where the drinking age was still eighteen, going too fast, he missed a curve on a wet country road and rolled the Buick three times. It only recently occurred to Carl that surviving the wreck was something like a miracle. The car was totaled. Carl and Bruce were both thrown free. Carl awoke half-buried in the wet soil and corn stubble, staring up at a fingernail moon and the white blur of the milky way arcing across the night sky. It took him some time to remember who and where he was. When he pulled himself up from the muddy field, he saw the twisted ruin of the Buick upside down above him, its headlights still dimly reaching out into the darkness. He felt as if he had died. Bruce lay back in the ditch, still drunk, and laughing. Laughing like an idiot.

A lifetime later, Carl saw an ad in the paper for a restorable Buick Gran Sport, and it seemed like the answer to something. His desire for the car was more need than want, and he borrowed from the savings account for Angel's college to get it. There was a long bad time with Gloria over that.

An almost full can of Old-Style sweats just beyond Carl's reach. He picks up the half inch ratchet handle with the extension and carefully extends it toward the beer can. He feels the pain in his chest again, and he lets the ratchet fall. He turns his head slightly and looks up to Miss February, still blessing the threader.

A small crack of sound in the distance. At Wrigley Field, a baseball arcs high away from a swung wooden bat. The sound of Harry Carey's voice rises in volume and intensity. Carl holds his breath, hoping that it means good news for the Cubs, a homer, runs scored at the least, a game-winning rally. But he can't make out the words, and the sound subsides to a low murmur, color commentary, the lull between batters. For Carl, the long fly ball continues to hang in the sky, its flight unresolved.

When he has calculated the reach, the foot-pounds of pull required to slide the can across the floor without tipping it, he again grasps the ratchet handle, reaches out and slowly draws the can toward him with the care of a master machinist.

When Carl has the can in his hand, he revels in its cool wetness a moment before tipping it over his mouth. Beer spills down his chin and soaks into his shirt as he drinks. He thinks again about lunch. The fried chicken left over from last night is in the refrigerator. He likes leftover fried chicken.

He can see out the garage door a square of driveway, his mailbox, the top half of the duplex across the street, blue sky above. The Shelby kid rolls by delivering papers from a skateboard. The Saturday Tribune skips across Carl's drive and into the holly bush. He almost yells after at the kid but decides against it. This is not the time to get into it with the paperboy. Carl wonders where Gloria is now. *How long can a person shop?* He knows that in Gloria's case unfortunately, the answer is a long goddamn time. He closes his eyes. The faint murmur of the ball game continues in the distance. The long fly ball still soars deep in center field. The clock on the wall whirs. Down the street a dog barks. And he hears footsteps coming down the sidewalk.

Carl holds his breath. The footsteps stop, and then start up again, coming closer. The footsteps come up the driveway. He opens his eyes. In the narrow gap between his feet and the gas tank of the Buick, he sees a pair of legs, faded blue jeans, athletic shoes, one untied, shuffling toward him. Not Bruce, he hopes. But it is Bruce, and now he hears the chuckle, low and suggestive. The sharp slap of an open hand on the top of the Buick.

"The fuck you doing under there?" says Bruce.

"What do you think?"

"Taking a nap?" Bruce laughs. "Huh huh."

"Maybe." *Maybe I'm dreaming*, thinks Carl, under his car.

"Listening to the Cubs?" says Bruce.

"Yeah."

"Yeah?" Carl imagines Bruce looking around, seeing the radio on the workbench, unplugged for the cord to the trouble light. The light hangs from the underside of the open hood, hooked into one of the ram air induction scoops, and it casts a yellow light down around the big block V-8. Carl, with the exception of his right arm, is in the shadows.

"I was," says Carl. "A while ago."

"I couldn't stomach it neither. Got no pitching at all this year." Bruce belches, and shuffles over to the workbench. Carl can see the back of his head as he leans over to get a closer look at Miss February.

"Wouldn't mind running some pipe through that threader." Bruce whistles. "Know what I mean."

"What do you mean, Bruce?" Carl says sharply.

"You know, man. I mean…"

"Forget it. I know what you mean."

"What's up? You sound kind of weird like."

"Yeah?"

"You need a hand?"

"No. I'm thinking."

"Thinking about what?"

"This tranny…"

"Turboglide, right?"

"Yeah."

"Them are good trannys."

"Yeah."

All I have to do is ask him to roll that floor jack back under here, Carl thinks, *and we could get this thing up enough for me to get out from under it*. But for some reason, he can't ask. He and Bruce went to high school together, played on the conference champion baseball team together, even dated a couple of the same girls. Carl remembers Bruce bragging once about tearing the clothes off that skinny little Muldowney girl in the bushes at a keg party, how she was so drunk she couldn't walk or talk. And Carl remembers not saying anything and he has never forgotten this.

Carl remembers sitting up in a muddy field and staring at the wreck of his car, feeling like his life was over, and Bruce's laughter ringing in his ears. *That was what, twenty years ago? Christ*, he thinks.

"I'm going to the Tap. Come with and have a cold one," Bruce says. He squats down and peers under the car at Carl, squints at him there in the shadows under the Buick.

Carl looks at the big, sideways face of his old friend and feels a powerful urge to flail at it with the heavy ratchet that lays by his hand. The urge is to hurt. To cause bodily harm. He takes a deep breath. Exhales.

"Nah. I'm in the middle of this here ..."

"Tranny?"

"Yeah."

"Anything you need before I go?"

Carl thinks about the cardboard bucket of fried chicken in the refrigerator, the cordless phone, which could be anywhere in the house, the Cubs game and the unplugged radio. He thinks, for no reason at all, about Angel.

"No," Carl says.

Bruce shuffles off down the driveway and down the street to the Tap where the usual crowd sits at their usual places at the bar, watching the Cubs win or lose another game. Gloria, meanwhile, browses through paperback classics at the Books-R-Us outlet. Carl, still under his car, hears from a couple blocks away the deep thumping of a high-power car stereo system with the bass pushed all the way up. A buzzing begins on the workbench as the thumping gets closer. The tools in Carl's garage begin to vibrate. Carl feels the low frequencies pulse through the transmission, through him, and through the concrete slab on which he lies. That Puerto Rican kid that Angel's been seeing, no doubt.

The kid drives a gleaming old Chevy Impala low rider with thirteen coats of hand-rubbed candy-apple lacquer, a trunk full of Die Hards and one of those hydraulic lift kits that drops the chassis down to within inches of the pavement and causes the car to hop up and down obscenely at stop-and-go lights. Carl can tell by the clatter of lifters from under the hood, and the blue-black smoke from the tailpipe that the motor is on its last legs. He wonders what kind of person would paint a car that barely runs. The batteries and the shocks are likely worth more than the whole goddamn car. Stomach acid gurgles and threatens to rise in his throat.

He refuses to learn the kid's name. Ralph, he calls the kid. Or Rudie. Ra-hoolio, if he's in a good mood. What does Angel see in a skinny, sorry-ass kid with the crotch of his pants hanging down almost to his knees? She's asserting herself, Gloria tells him. Let them be. They're just kids. That's what worries Carl. He and Gloria were just kids, too. But they weren't this stupid. Were they?

The Impala bounces to a stop at the curb outside Carl's house. The kid knows enough to turn the music down here, but Carl can still hear the insistent, muted thump of it, and the buzz and rattle of door panels and window glass. A car door slams. Sneakers skipping up the sidewalk. Angel. The front door slams shut. Carl imagines her dropping her jacket on the floor in the hall. She will never learn. She runs to her room, maybe. He has always been uncomfortable there and will only stand in the doorway trying not to look too closely at anything in the fragrant, jumbled room. So much color and life. Carl hears water running through the pipes inside his house. Noises in the kitchen. The side door opens.

"Daddy?"

"That you, Angel?" Carl's voice breaks slightly.

"How's your car coming?"

"Fine, honey."

Carl can see her feet. Pink canvas high tops poised. Her jeans taper and end mid-calf, revealing a hands width of thin leg, the graceful curve of ankle below. Carl has a great and sudden desire to hug his daughter, to hold her tightly in his arms for a long, long time.

"Me and Raul are going to the park. To hang out, okay?"

She's lost to me, Carl thinks, and he feels his heart breaking, the weight upon it almost unbearable.

"Okay," he says.

Angel skips toward the open garage door, and the sun-drenched, dangerous world. Carl struggles to follow the pink shoes in their carefree dance away from him.

"Angel," he calls out.

She stops. Turns back, pink shoes pivoting. "Yeah?"

"Be careful, honey."

And then she is gone. Carl lies under his car, eyes closed. The clock whirs. The world outside turns. It is Saturday, and spring is near. At Wrigley Field, relief pitchers warm up in the bullpen. Carl breathes and tries not to think about anything.

* * *

Carl looks up and sees Miss February move. Her head turns slightly so that she is looking down at him. She continues to smile, but in her smile is a look of pity and tenderness that he has not noticed before. The pipe threader beside her turns slowly, whirs smoothly, masking the far away chatter of the Cubs game. Miss February steps down from the workbench and moves toward Carl, her bare feet gliding over the cold concrete. A warm glow fills the garage.

She bends down beside the Buick, reaches under the car toward him. Carl in turn reaches out to her, his right hand outstretched, seeking her touch with neither thought nor hesitation. His right hand. He stares at her, transfixed by the vibrant, tanned skin of her arm, her hand, her fingers. Flawless, he thinks. Impossible. She touches him lightly, and in her touch, Carl feels the sure knowledge that everything will be all right. He relaxes, and only then realizes that he has been holding tension in his body, fighting against the weight that is upon him. He gives in to it. Accepts it. And it is lifted from him.

* * *

Later, when the pilgrims arrive to kneel in Carl's garage at the shrine to Our Lady of Skokie, as Miss February is christened by the media, Carl drives to a bar in another neighborhood where no one knows him and watches the Cubs with strangers. The Buick sits home in his driveway in an arrested state of partial restoration, covered with a tarp. Gloria sits inside the garage door in an upholstered chair she brought out from the family room, making change, and crocheting another afghan, or a sweater for Carl. The pilgrims pay five dollars to kneel at Carl's workbench and pray to the Ridgid Tool calendar.

Some of them believe they see Miss February's smile broaden, a light brightening in her eyes, a slight, sympathetic downward nod of her head as she looks upon them, one hand on her erotic, virginal hip, the other on the holy threader. Some reverently touch the stain on the garage floor where Carl lay pinned beneath the Buick before he was saved by Our Lady. They anoint themselves with the slick trace of the transmission fluid that coats the tips of their fingers. Some purchase small souvenir wrenches adorned with an enameled picture of the Virgin Mary (after consulting with the parish priest, Gloria decides against using the image of Miss February on the souvenirs; a letter from the Ridgid Tool company threatens legal action if their calendar, or their model is used in any type of marketing campaign. The church itself withholds judgment on the alleged miracle, issuing an ambiguous statement confirming that God does indeed work in mysterious ways, and that anything that increases faith is good, whether or not it is officially miraculous).

Gloria takes the money to the Savings and Loan to deposit into the account for Angel's college education. For the first time in years, Carl and Gloria do not argue about money, or about Angel. Carl gives Angel his blessing to go on the trip to Washington, D.C. He sees her off to O'Hare and hugs her for a long time in the terminal while the rest of the kids crowd toward the boarding gate. Angel hugs him back.

Carl, back to work with his brother-in-law, threads pipe and daydreams. On the job site, Carl runs the threader with a new proprietary air. He savors the smell of the cutting oil, the faint metallic taste in the back of his throat. Sometimes he stands next to the threader with his hand on the filthy motor casing in the same manner in which Miss February stands beside her threader.

By August, the pilgrims will have dwindled away, or Gloria will be forced by the city council (already the neighbors are complaining about the traffic and parking) to close the shrine. The Buick, freshly painted and rebuilt, will be back in the garage where Carl will work on the interior. A new headliner, carpeting, the seats reupholstered. Carl will install a new radio himself. He has a glow-in-the-dark statue of the Sacred Heart of Jesus for the dashboard. He will take Gloria for a drive on a Saturday night in the fall, park by the lake where they can smell the water and hear the hush of it lapping at the beach. Tune an oldies station in low. Her head on his shoulder, her hand on his chest. Carl will close his eyes and feel what it is like to have everything he ever thought he wanted, and then realize that it somehow isn't like he imagined it would be. And still, it will be all right.

* * *

Or perhaps Gloria arrives home from the mall and walks into the garage, her arms filled with shopping bags. She sees Carl, under his car. She frowns at the tool calendar hanging above the workbench.

"Why's your calendar still on February?"

"Huh?" Carl, shaken from a bizarre reverie. "Gloria?"

"Are you all right?"

"Gloria . . ."

"Just a minute. I have to set these bags down before I drop something."

Gloria goes into the house and Carl hears her shoes click across the linoleum. The radio comes on. The Rolling Stones singing "You Can't Always Get What You Want." Carl hears Gloria singing along. Her voice gives him chills.

She will return soon. She will position the floor jack to lift the transmission up off him. She will stay calm. He has always admired her ability to handle a crisis.

In high school when the Weber kid almost drowned in the pool, when everyone else stood there staring at the limp body on the stark, white concrete, it was Gloria who rushed up, knelt down and breathed the life back into him. Carl thinks this might have been the moment when he fell in love with her. He remembers being paralyzed, the smell of chlorine, water running down his face, his chest, his legs. And the image of Gloria, her slim, graceful fingers clamped over Weber's nose, and spread flat on his thin chest. To place her mouth over his, in front of God and everyone. To breathe into him. Her wet hair flat against her head, clinging to her freckled shoulders. A drop of chlorinated water hanging off the end of her nose like a jewel. In between breaths she straightened up, counting, oblivious. Her bathing suit was blue. Her breasts, small and nearly perfect, rose and fell, and with them a new ache in Carl's chest. The desire to be saved by her. A wail from far off like a siren. Yes, Carl thinks. *That was the moment.*

Gloria will insist on calling an ambulance, and she will ride in the back with him. While he waits for her to return to the garage, he thinks to ask her to bring along the bucket of leftover fried chicken. He can see by the change in light out the garage door that the sun is setting. It will be dusk by the time an ambulance arrives. He imagines lying under a clean, white sheet on a stretcher, looking up at the reflections of the lights flashing on the roof of the ambulance.

The morphine is working. The IV drips slowly, each translucent drop hanging like a textbook curve ball before dropping down into the graceful tube that arcs into Carl's arm. The ambulance driver has the Cubs game on the radio, turned down low, under the static of the two-way radio. It's the bottom of the ninth, all tied up. José Cardinal steps up to the plate. My man, José, Carl cheers silently. Gloria sits beside him and holds a cold drumstick to his mouth. He takes a bite of the chicken leg, and chews slowly. The taste is incredible. Heaven. It's as if he has never truly tasted anything until this moment, and he thinks that maybe everything will be this incredible from this moment on, out from under his car, saved.

*　*　*

Or perhaps Carl, under his car still, thrown from the Buick as it rolled and flipped into a cornfield in northern Illinois on a cold night in February, 1978. In the terrible, suspended flight, he saw in flashes of vivid imagination his future, and all that it would have held, lived this life in the brief moments before he came to rest in the damp soil and corn stubble where he would lay pinned beneath the car he loved and had destroyed, thinking about his father, about Gloria and their plans together. He would wait for a beautiful woman to save him. An angelic woman filled with light who would reach out to him a graceful flawless hand, lift the heaviness weighing upon him, fill him with her miraculous breath, and raise him up, up, and up.

Accident

How do I say this? How to I put it into words? *I had a motorcycle accident on the way to work today*. That doesn't quite capture it. I'm a little shaken up. I'm struggling to say this. To find the words. *I survived a motorcycle accident*. This is true, and goes without saying, but I'm saying it. *I wrecked my motorcycle*. Again, true, but it's not completely wrecked, and I'm still alive. There is more to it than damage to the machine. None of these quite explain what happened. I was late for a meeting at work, riding down Mineral Point Road towards the stoplight at Speedway Road. A white Mustang in front of me braked for the yellow light. A light that I expected him to run. One which I intended to run right behind him. I braked hard. I went over the handlebars. I slid across the pavement. I don't remember hitting the pavement, only the sliding across. Afterwards, a series of other events occurred. I went to work. I tried to make sense of it all. The elapsed time was not great but I'm having trouble with the chronology. I suppose I was going too fast, hurrying to work to this meeting. There was sand on the road, an incline, the car braking suddenly. I'm shaken up a little still. I'm not actually shaking, now in this meeting, but I feel as if I might be shaking, like my hands might be shaking. I keep my hands occupied with a pen, removing the cap and putting the cap back on, rolling the pen around in my hand. I occasionally write notes on a memo pad, pointless things

I know are pointless even as I write them. This meeting is pointless. I consider announcing this, and the proximity of death. But I don't. I don't know how to say. I decide, fuck them. My accident is none of their damn business. I'm a little shaken up still. It happened suddenly, as accidents tend to happen. I experienced a range of emotions in what seemed like seconds though was in fact a longer period of time. In fact, I realize, the period of time that might be described as the accident is still happening. *The accident is still happening* I say to myself in this meeting, and it will likely continue throughout the day. I have no basis for saying this other than the fact that those words just occurred to me.

The Firmament

Under certain circumstances Mostert might, under different circumstances that is, have been mistaken for a homeless person or an English professor. He gave the appearance of being well-fed. He was pale, of indeterminate European descent and neither smartly dressed nor entirely in good health. The actual circumstances were these: Mostert expounding on automobiles as he invaded my office at the Institute of Marginal Utility. He entered speaking and dropped his bulk heavily into a chair. This visit was not the first by any means but unbeknownst to me at the time, it would be the last time Mostert made an appearance in my office in this, his usual way. Or perhaps I did know at the time or had some inkling. I honestly do not remember.

Mostert was possessed of a remarkable sense of self-importance. He occupied a lot of territory. As I recall, on this occasion he'd apparently begun talking as he entered my office, or perhaps he'd begun talking prior to his entrance. I can't be sure. Had he begun talking as he walked down the hall towards my office? Had he been talking all along, on the elevator which descended to my floor from his, had he begun talking at some much point earlier in the day, begun perhaps talking upon his arrival at the office? Or upon waking? Each of these scenarios seemed within the realm of possibility.

Mostert seemed to appreciate an audience, but he did not require one, and one got the sense that he held them in low regard. Audiences, that is. People in general and in the specific. He had appeared in my office in this way regularly, without invitation or warning, for years. He was not one to waste time with pleasantries or small talk, launching right into, or perhaps continuing, his discourse, his lecture, his diatribe. What to call his holding forth? Mostert's commentary only occasionally rose, or descended, to the level of conversation, and only when on occasion a response or a question might occur to me that seemed not unintelligent and also happened to coincide with a pause on Mostert's part. I might then interject. But this did not often happen.

Mostert did not suffer fools. Or more accurately, he notified fools to their faces in no uncertain terms of the grief they caused him and the full extent of his disdain for them. I have to admit I admired him for this. And he happily disparaged them to me behind their backs, which was admittedly less admirable. Mostert considered most everyone a fool and I suspect he considered me a fool as well, though perhaps a more tolerable or convenient fool. Or perhaps I am only fooling myself. As a wise man allegedly once said, better to keep your mouth shut than to remove all doubt. I tend to leverage the doubt. I've been told I'm a good listener. In conversation I tend to keep my mouth shut and nod and make an agreeable humming sound that I imagine might be interpreted as encouragement.

I suspect, therefore, that I might appear more intelligent than I am, or more intelligent than I would if I were to open my mouth and try to articulate something on a topic such as twentieth-century military strategy or luxury automobiles or human resources, to name the top three areas of

Mostert's interest and expertise, areas about which he frequently dropped into my office to expound upon. By human resources, I mean specifically the gaffes, character flaws, and inferior intelligence of our colleagues at the Institute.

Whether his visits were for my gratification or education, or whether I was simply a convenient audience, I was never sure. I suspect the latter. I must admit that despite his demeanor and appearance, I felt a little pleased to have been apparently chosen, irregularly graced by his appearance, as it were, proof that I was a notch or two above the rest of the incompetents and fools, who were our colleagues, with perhaps one exception, at the Institute of Marginal Utility. I learned over time that he had an incautious fondness for Churchill and the opera, and for Kat, the assistant director of Marketing and Research.

It seemed at times that Mostert might have chosen me as a kind of protégé, dropping by my office on occasion to educate me on the fatal flaws of twentieth century military leaders, the latest options available on luxury automobiles, and the ever-expanding list of character flaws and missteps of the morons with whom we had to work at the Institute. Rain-sensing windscreen wipers, for example. Of course, it could have simply been that I tended to leave my office door open. I suppose he could also have been dropping in on other younger colleagues, straining their guest chairs with his bulk and holding forth about the same or perhaps slightly different topics, among which might easily be my own character flaws and gaffes and inferior intelligence. In the end I told myself this was unlikely and furthermore that I didn't care.

Regardless, Mostert's visits tended to leave me oddly unsettled, as well as behind on my workload, which was a concern for me. Rumors were circulating around the Institute of looming budget shortfalls, impending cutbacks, staffing measures, yet another restructuring. I had begun to consider other employment options. Mostert, however, had seniority at the Institute. He was entrenched and secure. He had connections. He bragged that he'd never retire, the job was so easy. There was some mystery concerning the particulars of his job. It was not entirely clear what exactly he did at the Institute, though to be fair this was not particularly unusual for his pay grade. Some believed that he had incriminating information on top administrators, which was not an unimaginable belief. Whatever the reason, the Institute seemed content to let Mostert be Mostert, a veritable ghost of the Institute past.

So, he would, on occasion, drop into my office whether I was in the middle of something or not. He never bothered to ask if it was a good time, if I was busy, if I had a minute. I would inevitably stop whatever I was doing, sit back, and listen. I'd nod and make my vague agreeable humming sound, and occasionally add a slightly cynical comment or a derisive laugh of my own, or rarely, an insightful question, if one happened to occur to me and I were feeling up to interjection.

Mostert preferred leasing to purchasing. He leased a new luxury car every year or two and spent much of his time researching the next luxury car he would lease as soon as the lease was up on the luxury car he was currently driving and whose deficiencies he meticulously documented. He appreciated cutting-edge engineering, precision and prestige, but most of all he prized roominess, vast interior spaces in which to stretch and luxuriate while hurtling down the road in the passing lane. He had been enamored with the

Germans for years, but after his last Mercedes, a cramped downsized redesign, he had sworn off Teutonic automobiles and made a swerve for the Brits. This may have been at a time when the Royals were in the news or perhaps a popular new BBC series on the class system.

But Mostert was no longer entirely happy with the British, he'd announced on a previous visit to my office. Yes, the Jaguar was faring better than the Benz, but he was looking ahead, deep into his research of the Japanese. A Lexus looked appealing. He'd been for a test drive the previous week and had been impressed, but for one glaring exception. He was appalled by the lack of head room in the Lexus.

Mostert was nearly as wide as he was tall. He spent much of his life seated and was unsteady on his feet. He lumbered down the halls of the Institute as if he were on the deck of a ship in rough seas, and slightly seasick. I smiled ever so slightly that day when Mostert said head room. No doubt the man required a roomy cabin, but head room? I wondered once again why I was the one with whom Mostert had chosen to share his automotive and military and institutional opinions.

I knew a little about cars myself, which may have been it. I was not a complete fool about the world beyond our adequate offices on the third floor of the Marketing and Research Building at the Institute. I'd done other things before accidentally becoming a marketing and research professional, including a stint in automotive maintenance and repair.

I drove a BMW myself, a used gray-market M5, a high-mileage rarity I'd had for years and that had seen better days. I'd purchased it from a Cuban chef and paid him in cash. He'd been smoking duck breasts in his garage the day

I picked up the car, and it smelled fabulous. Apple wood smoke, cigars and worn leather. The sedan was twenty years old and hardly the cutting-edge of the automotive world or even much to look at anymore. But it was not a bad car. It was a competent driving machine, something of a sleeper, a little banged up in the right front quarter and partly held together there with sheet metal screws and perforated metal strapping. But that's another story.

Suffice it to say, Mostert's visits inevitably involved opinions on cars and opinions on colleagues. The latter almost always tinged with disdain. But there was one exception, one visit during which Mostert revealed a side of his character that I had not imagined and have since found difficult to believe. Almost equidistant between my office and the elevator was the office of the long-time assistant director of Marketing and Research. Kat was an attractive woman at first glance, neither young nor old. She didn't quite fit at the Institute, yet she'd been there for years and looked younger each year. I'd heard mean-spirited colleagues whisper that she'd had work done, suggesting that her paid leaves involved plastic surgery of various kinds, medical tourism to South America and the like.

Kat kept a sofa in her office, and sometimes lounged on it drinking Diet Coke from a can. Whenever a young man was newly hired in Marketing and Research, Kat made it a point to show him around, to onboard him, in the parlance of Human Resources. Kat also took it upon herself to oversee the interns, bright young things from the local college. Some colleagues made off-color jokes behind her back, though not me and surprisingly, not Mostert.

I was never quite comfortable around Kat, though I got along with her alright. I was not her type, I suppose, too old for her, maybe, awkward with casual banter, and having apparently reached the peak of my career trajectory and begun the slow descent. It occurs to me that I never was inside Kat's office, which was a corner office, spacious, and as I mentioned, popular with the younger male colleagues and the interns.

Shortly after Kat died unexpectedly in Medellin, Mostert dropped into my office. He didn't look quite right, but it took me a while to realize what it was. He was talking about Kat, rambling in a voice strangely devoid of derision and critique. He went on for a while and then fell silent. He sniffled and looked at the floor. He was choked up! I realized. I was dumbfounded. Mostert, exhibiting compassion, or grief! Kat had been the only colleague about whom I'd never heard a negative word from Mostert. She was no dummy, but she would have fallen in the middle of the pack, intellectually, at the Institute. What was this? I wondered. What was the source of this uncharacteristic emotion?

It slowly dawned upon me like the sun gradually appearing along a distant horizon, the sky all glowing red, the ominous start of a new day. Mostert had liked Kat, and in a certain way. Had loved Kat? Had this love been requited? Un–? Consummated? Un–? So many questions arose. Of course, they were both married, though they only rarely, if at all, mentioned their spouses at work. Kat and Mostert had been at the Institute for decades together. Perhaps there had been a long-lost love, a past passionate indiscretion that pre-dated my employment.

I would learn nothing about their relationship from Mostert then or ever, and nothing about the details of Kat's unexpected demise which had occurred on a routine Colombian vacation. There was a brief memorial in the central hallway where a small conference table from one of the meeting rooms had been enlisted to showcase a framed glamour shot of Kat and testimonials from a few clients and colleagues printed on colored paper in a flowery typeface. There were a few books, odds and ends from her office, mementos for each of us to take away in remembrance.

Sebastian Nugent, the director of Marketing and Research, said a few somber and forgettable words. There was a moment of awkward silence. Gradually people drifted away to their cubicles and offices. Mostert lingered at the table. He picked up the photo of Kat and held it as if it were a rare and holy book and he were about to read from it. I averted my gaze and drifted away myself.

As the months passed, Mostert continued to drop by my office on occasion, though perhaps less frequently than before. And at some point, not long after learning about the lack of head room in the Lexus, I began closing my office door, which was frowned upon, though not strictly verboten as far as I could gather. I'd been at the Institute for quite a few years myself by then and I knew that though some of my colleagues might grumble and fuss to each other, nothing would come of it.

So, I began to close my door and complete my tasks free from Mostert's interruptions. Except for an occasional day when I had little or no work to do or was simply bored. On those days, I'd leave my office door open as if welcoming an intrusion. Sometimes Mostert would appear and other times not. I can't say that I was ever disappointed when he did not appear. I can't say that I was ever entirely pleased when he did walk in and drop heavily into a chair. I was ambivalent, mildly curious. I guess you could say his uninvited visits were part of the scenery, they were part of the job.

Then one day I was offered a new job at a more reputable institute. The Institute had seemed for years to be declining towards what seemed an inevitable denouement and I'd send out an application now and then. The more reputable institution was robust, it was expanding, it was all about growth and revenue. It meant for me more money and a slightly larger office on the seventh floor of a slightly larger building in a newer part of the city. My new office had a better view, to the southeast a sliver of lake glimmered beyond subsidized housing and the old hospital. To the southwest I had a birds-eye view of one of the most dangerous intersections in the city.

I gave two weeks' notice to Sebastian Nugent. I told a couple other people at the Institute that I was off to greener pastures. The janitor, whom I'd known for years, and with whom I occasionally shared a smoke outside the service entrance. The cheerful woman at the coffee kiosk who knew my preferences and routines. They understood, I think. Everyone was looking to get out of the Institute in those days and by the time I left, most of the old-timers were long gone. Except Mostert, of course. He would go down with the ship and its skeleton crew. Nugent as well, who had his eye on the next step up the administrative ladder.

On my last day at the Institute of Marginal Utility, I parked my battered Beamer on the top floor of the parking ramp. As I exited the elevator, I saw a sparkling new Lexus angled rakishly into the handicapped parking spot, well over the line. Mostert's new lease, it dawned on me. I paused to glance inside the lightly tinted windows. I admired the soft leather upholstery, the faux woodgrain steering wheel and accents. It seemed to have plenty of head room.

I went up to the third floor. I closed my office door and began packing up. I filled a cardboard box with flotsam from the office. A dusty softball league trophy. A few books and framed photos (*The Prince, Last Evenings on Earth*, my ex-wife and son, The Irish-Italian Softball Club), and an unlabeled cassette tape I'd pocketed on impulse at Kat's memorial. A pint bottle of Old Crow I kept in the file cabinet, half empty. My Institute-issued laptop and a few notepads and nice rollerball pens with the Institute logo. The box was nearly full and sufficient, I decided. I'd leave the rest. Let the next occupant sort it out.

I looked one last time out the window at my old view of the parking garage beyond the sorry little quadrangle with its abstract Corten steel sculpture, a rusting misshapen orb that memorialized and outlasted a previous CEO and his disastrous restructuring plan. From my third-floor vantage I could see Mostert's Lexus half in the shadows, still occupying the handicap spot. I considered opening the office door in case he might happen to drop by one last time, but did not. I sat for a moment in my chair with my feet up on the empty desk. I tried unsuccessfully to muse about the past and the future. With my hands behind my head, I imagined I looked carefree, like someone awaiting their next looming adventure.

I imagined Mostert dropping his bulk into the chair, launching right into, or perhaps continuing, his discourse on the Maginot Line or the pious ineptitude of Sebastian Nugent, who drove a Prius, or the surprisingly adequate head room of the Lexus. Or perhaps confessing once and for all his profound love for Kat, though he had never again mentioned her after the memorial.

Mostert was among the many colleagues whom I had not notified of my new position and my departure from the Institute. It had frankly not occurred to me. We'd been colleagues almost twenty years, which was hard to believe. I could, I thought, walk by Mostert's office on my way out, drop in on him for a change, say good-bye and such. I realized that I'd never been inside Mostert's office, which was the only office at the far end of a long windowless hall on the third floor. He took the elevator up to the fifth floor for meetings, and I imagine, to drop in on me. And perhaps on Kat as well. I couldn't picture Mostert's office, Mostert in his office, or what I'd have to say to him.

I picked up the cardboard box and opened the door. The coast was clear, as they say. I took the stairs down and went out the back of the building. I paused at Mostert's new Lexus, its calfskin upholstery, generous head room, etc. Its invisible yet inevitable deficiencies not yet apparent. I shifted my grasp on the cardboard box and walked on. I took the stairs to the top of the parking ramp, where I liked to park. I like the feeling of the firmament above me, the flat city laid out before me like evening on a table is in that poem, the vista from there beneath it. The firmament, that is.

I put the cardboard box in the trunk. I stretched my arms above my head into the dank air of a Friday afternoon and luxuriated in the moment. There were thoughts and emotions, deep and inarticulate. The eternal footman and growing old and so on. Finally, I slid behind the wheel. I opened the sunroof and revved the engine. I had no quarrel with German engineering. I slid a cassette into the tape deck, an unmarked C-90 that had caught my eye on the table of mementos at Kat's memorial. I turned up the volume and the car was filled with strange music.

I drove out of the parking garage for the last time, a little faster than usual, with reckless abandon, as my high school football coach would say, the tires squealing in complaint around the corners, the eerily mournful music filling the cabin and from the open windows echoing in the nearly empty garage. And as I drove away, I glanced in the rearview mirror at the Marketing and Research Building, small and growing smaller behind me. I imagined Mostert in shirt sleeves, leaning at the windowsill or taking the elevator up to the fifth floor and walking past Kat's old office, past the closed door of my former office, and then past Kat's old office door once more on his way back towards the elevator. He would have no idea. Had he begun talking already? He would keep walking, his odd and awkward walk, wallowing past the closed office doors, but to where? Back to his office hidden away on the second floor? Or would he find another open office door? Would he walk in uninvited and drop his bulk into another chair and launch into his discourse, the same or another?

It was truly a mystery then to me what Mostert might do, and it remains a mystery to this day. I decided while driving away from the Institute that going forward I would close the door while at work in my new office there on the seventh floor at the more reputable institution that awaited me. And so, I drove away from Mostert and his memories of Kat, away from the offices and the workload, the administration and the coffee kiosk and abstract Corten steel sculpture, away from the Marketing and Research Building, the details of the people and the place blurring and fading away with every passing block. I recall driving down the avenue that day toward a future of possibilities, joyfully weaving the battered old driving machine around potholes to a narcocorridoes soundtrack, the sunroof open and above the old trees, the wide whitewashed sky hanging above me like an unwritten page.

I admit that I have similar memories of driving down that oak lined avenue, memories which may have become conflated with this particular memory. For instance, once in a friend's convertible sports car, passing by the Institute in late July, and another time driving the same stretch of macadam as a streetcar in a fleeting scene from Lolita, the later adaptation with Jeremy Irons, passed us by. It occurs to me that these are all scenes that I recall clearly, perhaps the only ones, scenes in which the crumbling street rolls slowly beneath the tires, the unconcerned sky yawning above, all scenes I seem to recall more clearly than if I had been there.

Sour Diesel

I guess I knew that Michigan was one of the states that had legalized recreational marijuana, but I hadn't given it much thought since I had not lived in Michigan in many years and had not used marijuana recreationally in years either. Except a few times, including at Jazz Fest a year or two after Katrina when I'd bumped into a woman I knew, a realtor, in the crowd at the Congo Square stage. She was a little insane like we all were at that time. As we swayed to the beat beneath the white-hot Louisiana sun, she produced a joint and held it up like a sacrament. She lit it, took a hit, tipped her head back, and released a great euphoric cloud of smoke that hung in the air above us. She offered the joint to me, and I accepted it without thinking. I took a big hit like we used to back when. It had been years and this weed was different than the weed I remembered. I felt a little paralyzed. I felt the earth slowly rotating in space and for a moment I was afraid I might lose consciousness. I'd been drinking beer of course in the heat, and I realized later I was probably dehydrated too. I made my way through the crowd and lay down in the grass by a fence for a while until I felt I could go on. So that had cured me for a while, until recently when I began thinking again about cannabis, feeling the old desire, and curiosity. It cured me, that is, until I traveled to Detroit for the funeral of a friend.

After the funeral I drove around in the rental car. I had nowhere else to be. I thought about going down to Wyandotte, an old friend's hometown she'd told me about. She'd described it to me such that I felt like I knew it. I could picture it as if I'd been there before. Then I thought about Tiger Stadium. I had actually been to Tiger Stadium, but my recollection of it was hazy, as if it had been in a dream. In a way, it was less real to me than Wyandotte.

I was not looking for a dispensary, but I got turned around while searching for the site of old Tiger Stadium, which of course has been torn down. I'd been there as a kid when the city was still smoldering from the riots in 1968 after the assassination of Martin Luther King Jr. It was perhaps the only baseball game my father ever took me to. He drove us into the city in our Acapulco Blue Ford Country Sedan station wagon. We rolled in stunned silence, wide-eyed white suburbanites, past burned-out block after burned-out block, past abandoned cars without wheels up on concrete blocks. I thought of photos I'd seen of post-War Europe and of *Slaughterhouse Five*, which I'd recently read in trade paperback. The stadium rose up from all that the destruction around it like a cathedral or a coliseum.

I remember walking around inside Tiger Stadium with the massive iron beams and the distant green manicured field where Mickey Lolich, Al Kaline, Willie Horton, and the rest threw a small bright white baseball around. Intoxicated with the smells of popcorn and steamed hot dogs and beer, I wandered the concourse, swinging a souvenir baseball bat. The decline of the auto industry and of Detroit itself was right around the corner.

As I drove around years later, looking for the site of Tiger Stadium, I did not know that Al Kaline would be dead in a matter of months, at age 85, the same age as my father. When finally I drove in disbelief past the empty expanse where Tiger Stadium used to be, I could not quite believe it was gone, or even that it had been possible to tear it down. But clearly it had been torn down and nothing of it remained. I got out of the car and walked out to where I imagined first base might have been. I stepped out from the baseline onto the infield. I turned and crouched, looking toward home plate. I pounded my fist into my palm. I squinted toward the batter, ready for the pitch. There was only the white noise of the freeway, seagulls circling above a huge vacant lot. I knelt down and scooped up a handful of the dry, red sandy soil and closed my first around it. I walked back to the car with the fistful of dirt. I emptied a Ziploc baggie of Advil onto the terrace, poured the dirt into the baggie, sealed it, and tucked it into my carry-on.

I drove on to Woodward Avenue, to the site of the Algiers Motel, which I discovered had also been torn down. I sat in the car looking across the empty green space for a while, trying without success to imagine the neighborhood as it had been in the late sixties. In Detroit, as in New Orleans, I was conscious of being a white man in a black city, though a little less at ease than I once was. All I could conjure up were black-and-white news photos and dark scenes from a movie. I drove on until I saw a red brick building on a corner with a sign that read Corktown Collective. I was in Corktown, Detroit's old immigrant Irish neighborhood. Illuminated green crosses beckoned in the first-floor windows. I parked the rental car out front.

The store was brightly lit, sparely furnished with a big convex security mirror and a glass display case behind which stood a young white woman with blonde dreadlocks and an eye-catching nose piercing that glinted like a lure in the overhead light. She was wearing yoga pants and a hoodie and smiling hugely. I smiled back and might have felt almost at ease, if it had not been for the startling image of a gray-haired old man, who might have been fresh from a funeral, there above me in the security mirror. The young woman brought out samples on a tray that she placed carefully on the top of the glass case. It was like shopping for an expensive wristwatch or a handgun. I leaned forward with my hands clasped innocently behind my back, to examine the wares. She explained the various varieties, the hybrids, about terpenes, aromas and flavors, medicinal uses, and overall effects.

The young woman had a wristband of Rasta-colorful knotted twine, and a small Celtic knot tattooed on the fleshy part of her hand, between her thumb and forefinger. It looked like she chewed her fingernails, and as I gazed at her thin hand, I felt an urge to reach out and take it in mine. I flashed back to my old friend from Wyandotte who'd had a similar tattoo on the back of her shoulder. Not unlike the Celtic cross inked on my left arm. My arm then performed an involuntary movement, the shoulder rolling and creaking, the hand flexing slightly, cracking, the arm raising slowly as if to say, I don't know what.

There'd been a time in Knoxville, another life or two ago, a crawfish boil, late summer, right off Thunder Road. There'd been an impulsive late-night run to Mountain Tattoo. Back in Corktown I heard myself exhale and I opened my eyes. I smiled reassuringly at the young woman, with maybe a touch of wistfulness. I returned to the tray of samples and marveled at the presentation, the names and the intricacies of the aromatic flowers. White Widow. Afghan Kush. Sour

Diesel. It was a little overwhelming. Supernatural. Northern Lights. I felt the old hunger for herb, a longing like nostalgia for wasted days couch-locked in a cheap clapboard rental with a massive Marantz, centerpiece of a vintage hi-fi altar, vinyl spinning without end, the sacrament passing from hand to hand around the smoke-filled room. So much lost and wasted and yet now more sweet than bitter it seemed, in the wake of another funeral. I glimpsed my own gray visage again, a ghost up there floating distorted in the security mirror behind the counter.

I asked about Sour Diesel. I liked the name. It's good for depression and stimulating creativity, the tattooed young woman told me. There's an aroma of sour lemon, she said, with just a hint of like gasoline. She held out a bud gently cradled in her slim fingers. I closed my eyes and inhaled. Yes, I said. I think I see. A typically sativa cerebral hit that comes on fast, she said. It seemed like just what I might need. I went with Sour Diesel, purchased a gram, a little in disbelief of the legal and brightly lit over-the-counter transaction. Sour Diesel was, I hoped, the fuel I'd need to carry on. I drove to a marathon station where I topped off the gas tank and bought a souvenir Tigers t-shirt. I rolled the package of Sour Diesel into the t-shirt and shoved it into my carry-on. My heart beat a little faster. I started the rental car and drove, following the signs, merging onto 1-94, aiming for the airport, leaving Michigan again, hoping for the best.

The New Species

I have been unable to sleep since the discovery of the new species. Each night I retire more exhausted than I was the night before, determined to sleep, and yet each night my mind grapples with, in addition to the usual nightmares of nightbirds and assembly lines, with wild imaginings of the new species. My thoughts circle the creature-like fictional planets and cosmic debris whirling around a minor sun in a faraway galaxy. By the time dawn crawls above the ashen horizon I once again arise unrested and further deranged by the new species. I pack my lunchbox and go to work. I daydream at my post in the factory, the third quality inspection engineer near the end of line. I try to reassure myself that this new species is likely nothing more than a rare variant of the old species, a suspicion I hope to confirm when I finally could see it for myself. Oswald is keeping the new species in his basement. He's agreed to let me see it on Saturday. This knowledge and anticipation do not remedy but only amplifies my insomnia and Saturday is still three days away. I am concerned that my sanity might not abide that long. Oswald told me about the new species perhaps a week ago and I am now five or seven or perhaps nine days without sleep. To be honest I'm not at all sure. He confided to me that he discovered the new species in the partial shade of his garden. He captured it with a large landing net and a lawn chair, he said, surprising it among the root vegetables and the psylocibin mycelium he cultivates on a length of dead tree trunk from a pin oak we dragged back there after the company cleared the last scrap of nature to expand the neighborhood for housing to accommodate an additional shift at the factory. Oswald has assured and reassured me that the new species is well and safe and healthy. He has it securely chained to his furnace and when I call him on the cellular, I can hear in the background disturbing noises that seem consistent with furnaces and chains and a lively new species. Oswald insists that the new species is not yet acclimated and therefore it will be best to wait until Saturday to see it. I do not entirely believe Oswald, nor have I ever fully trusted him after the disappearance of the pharmacist who used to live across the street in a house painted in Electric Blue Mist, which was the closest to a primary color anywhere in the neighborhood, a color which may have since been discontinued. Certainly, none of the houses in the new subdivision are painted in Electric Blue Mist. As the minutes and hours pass by, it gradually becomes clear to me, as if a strange and familiar voice is whispering somewhere in my head. I cannot wait until Saturday to see the new species. Not necessarily a voice whispering those exact words, or even words at all, but the thought of it, the notion that I cannot wait manifests itself inside my head. The notion to mosey over to Oswald's late tonight soon follows. These are the considerations, the scheme as it occurs to me. We—I and Oswald and most of our neighbors—we punch the time clock at the factory at 5 p.m. every weekday and we each retire to our prefab company houses, each of which is distinguished by color and landscaping. My house came from the factory painted in Blue Steel Barrel, a sinister color slightly towards the left side of the blue-gray continuum. A sickly locust tree is staked in the hardpacked ash-covered lawn. Oswald's house several doors down came equipped with an Old Gray Mare exterior, several shades darker on the west end of the continuum and every bit as mysterious as you might expect from its name. As if that were not enough, Oswald's front yard features a persistent Dutch elm of which I am envious. At home alone after work we consume TV dinners and Grain Belt beer in aluminum cans and watch extremely short videos on company-issued handheld devices. Some nights I call Oswald on my device or Oswald calls me on his. Previously these calls might cover such topics as TV dinner entrée choices, sides, or desserts, the death of God, extremely short videos that have recently amused us, ice hockey or mixed martial arts. But for the past week there has been little discussion of food or videos or combat sports. All we talk about it seems is the new species. I, for one, can think of nothing else. The new species has taken hold of my imagination and will not let go. Unlike me, Oswald sleeps like the dead each night, turning in at 10 p.m. as regular as a piston. So I figure if I happen to take a late walk, make my way down the street about 11 or midnight, it will be nothing at all to then mosey into the alley alongside Oswald's gray house, to stop and look around for a moment before crouching down to peer into the small rectangular window set in the concrete foundation there beside a red wheelbarrow with a flat tire. So much depends upon timing. I'll be wearing dark clothing of course. Wiping the filthy glazing with my dark sleeve, the glass will be cleared more or less of spiderwebs and of the omnipotent ash from the factory that troubles the lungs. I'll cough quietly into my elbow as we've been trained to do. My eyes will take a moment to adjust to the quasi-darkness of Oswald's basement, the small orange cyclops glow in the furnace door that I imagine is the only available light. Upstairs prone in his bed, drifting along in the dreamless sonata of the dead will be Oswald. I'll wait for a few moments, savoring the anticipation. Isn't it, after all, also about the waiting? Waiting for the right moment? The shifts will have changed at the factory and the nightly contest between the old neighborhood team and the new team will be reaching its crisis. I might hear sirens in the distance, perhaps the security forces rushing to the scene of a fatal intersection mishap on the main thoroughfare or to the Rungradito, the company stadium, to break some skulls. I listen motionless in the shadows to the sirens becoming louder and then fading and fading further and diminishing into the relative silence (insects quietly humming and chirping, the trees feebly exhaling oxygen, the rest of the first shift in their small houses distantly tossing and turning and mumbling in their restless sleep, one or the other of them occasionally crying out or muffling cries in standard-issue foam pillows, somewhere nearby a nocturnal raptor suddenly leaving the branch with an audible sweep, intent on its oblivious prey). I gaze into the window and finally I see it there yet not quite there beside Oswald's furnace. I see its eyes and they lock onto mine and it looks at me as I look at it in startled recognition, the new species. At which point I expect I will wander home and begin finally to drift away into a deep and dreamless slumber.

Fair Oaks Diner

This story begins with a rusting white sign on a brick building spelling the word EAT in red neon, and as I'm driving past, the gravitational pull of it causes me to parallel park my truck out front. Also, it's snowing. This story is an acquaintance of a story called "American Flag Decal" by Richard Brautigan, though that story would likely deny this if the two stories would happen to meet in a perfectly ordinary diner like this one where an old radiator is battling winter like a punch-drunk boxer who won't stay down. I order coffee and eggs and toast and hash browns. I've driven past this diner more times than I can count, resisting the sign, but now here I am at the counter drinking black coffee and waiting on my order. I heard an old friend's sister-in-law owns this place and I think how I might say to her, *Hey, I knew your sister-in-law twenty-five years ago in St. Paul.* But the only person behind the counter is a guy who looks like a junior heavyweight who's intently wishing he were someplace else, like maybe San Diego. I can't see who's in the kitchen, so I content myself with the coffee and waiting and yesterday's newspaper. The only other characters are two retired guys at a table, regulars I guess, since the junior heavyweight knows their names. I picture another story, yet unwritten, where I'm an old sportswriter who comes in every morning and they all know my name and stories. Behind the counter a WINSTON SALEM display for packs of cigarettes sits sad and empty, the space inside like a small museum of the days when you could smoke in gymnasiums and in diners with your coffee while you waited for your order to come up. There are two different clocks on the wall, each with its own different version of time. Finally, here it comes, the junior heavyweight carries a plate piled with eggs, toast, and hash browns. He sets down the plate and refills my coffee. The story ends as I dig in and begin to eat. It's not the best eggs and toast and hash browns I've ever had but there's plenty, and there's hot sauce. As I eat, I see through the window the red glow from the sign on the falling snow and on my truck waiting patiently for the page to turn.

Acknowledgments

Thanks to the editors of these publications where earlier versions of these stories appeared:

"On Montegut Street" in *Green Mountains Review*
"Meatcutter" in *Notre Dame Review*
"My Sylvie, Her Paradise" in *Washington Square*
"Scar Baby" in *Pindeldyboz*
"Take the Wheel" in *Washington Square*
"The Velvet Underground" in *Quarterly West*
"Laundry" in *The Normal School*
"Postal" in *Fourteen Hills*
"Memphis" in *Fiction Southeast*
"Vulcan" in *Portland Review*
"O Happy Living Things" in *Short Fiction*
"Summertime" in *French Quarter Fiction*
"Engaged to Death" in *Diagram*
"New Mexico" in *Jelly Bucket*
"Carl, Under His Car" in *The Gettysburg Review*
"The Firmament" in *North Dakota Quarterly*
"The New Species" in *The Talking River Review*
"Fair Oaks Diner" in *Madison Magazine*

Thank you to the National Endowment for the Arts for their support, and to the many good teachers, students, readers, writers, and friends who helped along the way, including David Carr and Ian Graham Leask in Minneapolis; Michael Martone, Lex Williford, Richard Rand, and too many more to mention in Alabama; Michael Jeffrey Lee, Pia Erhardt, Anne Gisleson, Robert Bell, and Mary McCay in New Orleans; and CX Dillhunt, Steve Verburg, Deb Smith, Madeline Uranek, and Andy Millman in Madison. Finally, thanks to Grace Dahl, Amanda Leibham, Dr. Ross Tangedal, and the rest of the staff at Cornerstone Press for turning it into a book.

CHRISTOPHER CHAMBERS is the author of *Delta 88*, a small book of short prose, and *Inter/views*, a book of poetry. He is co-editor (with Peyton Burgess) of the anthology, *Ice Fishing for Alligators*, and his work has been published widely in magazines and anthologies including *Best American Mystery Stories*, *The Normal School*, *BOMB Magazine*, and *The Southern Review*.

He was born in Wisconsin and has since lived in North Carolina, Michigan, Minnesota, Florida, Alabama, Texas, and Louisiana. He's worked as a farmhand, a carpenter, and a lifeguard. He's worked in a warehouse, a slaughterhouse, and in an English Department. He's repossessed cars. He's an erstwhile Teamster and he's given up tenure. He's back in Wisconsin where he works as a bartender, an editor, and teaches in a state prison.

www.ingramcontent.com/pod-product-compliance
Lightning Source LLC
Chambersburg PA
CBHW031525310726
48971CB00008B/2359